SIRENS OF DUNKIRK

Sirens of
Dunkirk

Leo Kessler

This first world edition published in Great Britain 2003 by
SEVERN HOUSE PUBLISHERS LTD of
9–15 High Street, Sutton, Surrey SM1 1DF.
This first world edition published in the USA 2003 by
SEVERN HOUSE PUBLISHERS INC of
595 Madison Avenue, New York, N.Y. 10022.

British Library Cataloguing in Publication Data

Kessler, Leo, 1926-
  Sirens of Dunkirk
  1. Intelligence officers - Great Britain - Fiction
  2. World War, 1939-1945 - Secret service - Great Britain - Fiction
  3. War stories
  I. Title
  823.9'14 [F]

  ISBN 0-7278-5884-X

Except where actual historical events and characters are being
described for the storyline of this novel, all situations in this
publication are fictitious and any resemblance to living persons
is purely coincidental.

Typeset by Palimpsest Book Production Ltd.,
Polmont, Stirlingshire, Scotland.
Printed and bound in Great Britain by
MPG Books Ltd., Bodmin, Cornwall.

The game of espionage is too dirty for
anyone but a gentleman.

British Intelligence Officer, 1940

PRELUDE:
A KNOCKING SHOP IN DUNKIRK

S ome people can't pour piss out of a boot if there wasn't instructions on the frigging heel, the Old Sweat told himself sourly as the Bedford truck pulled up in front of the knocking shop. Aloud he said, 'Here we are, Corp, randy and ready for a bit o' the other.'

The young signals corporal, with his fresh innocent face, looked worried. 'We're not supposed to, you know, Nobby. They'll put us on a charge if we're caught. You know how keen the General is to stamp out VD in the Third Div.'

The Old Sweat took it in his stride. He'd been breaking King's Regulations for over fifteen years now. 'Frig the General, VD and the Third Div.,' he said easily. 'When a bloke's got a stiff one like I have at this moment, he don't worry about them kind o' things. Yer know what they say, Corp – an erection ain't got no conscience.' He laughed, displaying his yellow false teeth. 'I've been here before, Corp, last time we was sent to Dunkirk. It ain't the best knocking shop I've bin in –' at the back of his brain a cynical little voice rasped to himself, and Nobby, old lad, you've bin in more knocking shops than frigging Corporal Blenkinsop here has had good dinners – 'but them French tarts do give yer a good working over, I must admit.' He licked his lips as if in anticipation. 'Lovely grub.'

'But it's a shop,' the young corporal said, perhaps in an attempt to dodge the issue at hand.

'Just a front,' the Old Sweat answered easily. 'The port

authorities don't allow knocking shops in Dunkirk. Think they might corrupt us innocent *Anglais*.' He tapped the bulging breast pocket of his battledress, where lay the francs they had just earned on the local black market selling cannisters of Army petrol to the French. 'Come on, Corp. Let's get at 'em. We ain't got all day, yer know.' Without waiting for the young NCO, the old sweat moved forward, merrily singing, '*M'selle from Armentières . . . never been fucked for twenty years . . . inky-pinky, parlez-vous . . .*'

Reluctantly, the corporal followed, his face suddenly flushed a beetroot red with embarrassment. Standing at the top of the stairs, he had abruptly spotted a big blonde, her enormous bosom seemingly about to burst out of her dress at any moment. And as the Old Sweat called over his shoulder, 'That's Giselle . . . she never does wear drawers. Hairy, ain't she?', the young NCO could quite distinctly see that she wasn't a true blonde and was too embarrassed to reply.

A moment later Giselle was submerging Nobby's bald head in between those magnificent breasts while stretching out a hand towards the corporal, as if she desired him to kiss it, crying, 'Hello Tommy, you want good time? Much jig-jig?' She attempted to wink but her false eyelashes were that long she didn't manage it.

The corporal cringed. He prayed urgently that Giselle wouldn't embrace him; he didn't think he'd be able to stand it.

A few minutes later they had moved up the rickety stairs to Giselle's establishment, as she proudly called it, with the madame throwing out her pudgy hand and crying, '*Voilà*'.

The corporal gave a choking cough. The place stank of cheap scent, stale food, pungent French cigarettes and what he could only call to himself 'female parts', well-used female parts at that!

Cautiously he looked around, as the Old Sweat tried to get

his hands on those magnificent breasts – without success, as the madame exclaimed, 'No money – no jig-jig, *compris?*'

It was a large room, filled with overstuffed, plush furniture. On the walls there were pornographic photos everywhere, including two hefty, Eton-cropped naked females doing something to each other which made the corporal turn his gaze away hastily, plus a cross hung with rosaries with below it a large box of condoms.

The madame caught the direction of the red-faced NCO's gaze and said, '*Oui*, we are a clean house – you will see. No disease here. Always the French letter.' She smiled at him, revealing a mouthful of gold teeth.

The Old Sweat pulled a face. 'Not natural, it ain't, having to wear a raincoat,' he mumbled sourly. 'No pleasure in it for a bloke.'

The blonde ignored him. Instead she clapped her hands. 'My beauties will see you now.'

'I got my peepers on a pair of beauties already,' the Old Sweat said. But then he forgot the madame's ènormous breasts as her 'beauties' trooped in in a single line, one behind the other, like schoolgirls summoned to appear before a particularly strict headmistress and be introduced to parents who might put their own daughters into the school if they liked the look of the girls.

Not that they were in any way girls, the corporal told himself. Most of the whores seemed old enough to be his mother. The first was a hard-faced blonde who would never sce forty again. She was wearing high-heeled laced-up boots and a fading black corset. He supposed it was pulled so tight in order to lift up her wrinkled sagging breasts. If so, it failed lamentably. The blonde gave him a quick professional smile then yawned and began to scratch her naked pubic hair. Alarmed, he told himself that he wouldn't choose her; she probably had crabs.

'Bernice,' the madame introduced her. 'Very special. She

5

belong once to a Paris gentleman. Very old and rich.' She shrugged dramatically and her breasts rose up above the top of her dress like two huge balloons ascending. 'He need special treatment, you understand?'

As if she had been waiting for her cue, the whore slapped the lash, which she had attached to her wrist, wearily against her boot, and bared her teeth. But her raddled, roughened face conveyed nothing but weary boredom.

Still, the corporal wasn't impressed, but the Old Sweat was agitated, as if he couldn't get a woman, any woman, on her back with her legs in the air, soon enough; his need was so great.

But the madame was not to be hurried. She presented the next whore, and the next, while the Old Sweat kept patting her generous rump bulging through the tight black skirt as if he were judging its weight like some butcher prior to buying a prize heifer.

The corporal wasn't impressed by the whores; indeed if the truth were known, he was a bit frightened of them. They all looked so experienced and as if they would expect him to do things to them of which he hadn't a clue. At that moment he wished he was back at the NAAFI in Lille drinking a nice cup of tea and waiting to go into the pictures and see the latest Arthur Askey film which everyone said was so funny. Then the door to the inner room opened to let in yet another of the madame's beauties. She was much younger than the rest, pretty in what seemed to the corporal a dark foreign manner. She was clad in an open black artifical shift, which could have revealed a lot of her skinny body. But she didn't flaunt her nakedness like the rest. Instead she kept her hands in front of her jet black pubic hair and crouched a little so that she didn't reveal too much of her small, pink-tipped breasts. The corporal, telling himself she might be the one for him – she probably wouldn't make fun of him if he did anything stupid – thought she looked half-starved and worn out.

'Rachel,' the madame announced, adding as if she were imparting something very important, '*Juive* – Jewess.' She rolled her eyes melodramatically as she said, 'She near virgin.'

'How near—' the Old Sweat commenced.

The madame cut him short with a very businesslike, 'Show me money – then you pick.'

Hurriedly the Old Sweat reached for the greasy wad of francs in the top pocket of his battledress blouse. He handed it to the madame, who scanned the notes very professionally, tugging at the paper and holding a couple of them up to the red, dim light, presumably to check the watermark.

'*Bon*,' she concluded a moment later. '*Ça va*. You pick now.'

She didn't give the old soldier back the black market money, but the Old Sweat didn't seem to mind. His gaze was now fixed greedily on a redhead with breasts like enormous puddings; licking his lips all the time, as if he had suddenly become very hungry.

'I think I'll have her,' he said slowly, flashing a quick glance at the whore called Rachel. 'Perhaps you can throw her in as a reserve, madame – after all the lolly you've taken.'

The madame shook her head firmly. 'Specials –' she made the French gesture of counting notes with her thumb and forefinger – 'cost much money.'

The Old Sweat shrugged carelessly. 'All right, Ma. I get yer. I'll take the bint with the red hair.' He turned to the embarrassed corporal. 'You can have skinny Lizzie, then. Pant a bit and blow a bit o' hot air into her blouse. Them tits of hers wouldn't give a suck – and I said *suck* – to a well-fed infant. Ta ta.' He moved in on the redhead, his greedy paws already circling the dimpled globes and fatty buttocks.

7

'I say,' the corporal stuttered, 'you're not going to leave me on my lonesome, are you?'

'What d'yer want me to do, Corp, put you on her?' the Old Sweat sneered, a scornful look on his tanned wizened face. 'And by the way, you see that mirror on the ceiling of her room?'

'Yes. I wondered why there's a mirror up there,' the NCO answered, looking puzzled.

'Well, it's not for combing yer back hair, Corp.' He laughed, and grabbing the whore propelled her to her bedroom, crying over his skinny shoulder, 'Ta ta for now and don't do nuthin' I wouldn't do.'

Rachel closed the door behind him as he preceeded her into the bedroom. Immediately he commenced flushing again and felt even more of a fool because he was doing so. The girl stood next to the greasy washbasin with a small white hand towel and soap in her hand. 'You wash,' she said.

'Wash what –' he caught himself in time, realizing that there was only one part of the male body that would need washing in the 'knocking shop', as the old sweat called the place. He moved forward.

Down below in her 'office', a curtained-off section behind the cash register on the zinc-covered little bar, the madame was speaking urgently into the phone and she was not speaking French. In the harsh, guttural, unlovely Flemish of West Flanders she said, *'Ik kan niet komen . . . Nee . . . Ik heb . . .'*

At the other end the unknown speaker gave way. *'Ja, ja ik komme,'* he agreed. *'Tot ziens.'*

Urgently the gross brothel-keeper put the phone down and started to examine the first battledress blouse that the redhead had brought down to her when she had fetched the little towel. This was wartime and goods were short; the madame wanted to account for every towel, and especially soap which was rationed. With a practised hand, she opened the stiff brass buttons of the twin battledress pockets and started to examine their contents.

She already knew from the Tommies' black-and-red triangular patch that they belonged to the English Third Infantry Division, which was commanded by a certain General Montgomery. She knew, too, that this division was up at the frontier with neutral Belgium some thirty kilometres away, digging and building new fortifications as an extension to the Maginot Line. What she, and her masters, didn't know was what this Third Division would do if the Germans invaded through Belgium. It was one of her jobs to help to find this out . . .

It had been an exciting experience, indeed it had been the corporal's really first experience of 'going all the way'. Till then, it had been the girls back home with their severe and pretty prim 'Not past the top of my stockings, do you hear, or I'll slap your face, I promise you that.' Now he lay back on the rumpled bed and watched the girl in the ceiling mirror (now he knew what it was used for and it was certainly not for parting his hair!) as she rose from the bed and went over to the dirty sink to wash herself. With her skinny back to him, she spread her legs and started to soap her inner thighs busily.

She had been very 'nice' to him – he couldn't think of another word to describe her behaviour. When he had had difficulty in drawing on the contraceptive, she had helped him on with it and rubbed soap on the French letter to lubricate it and had whispered, 'Make it better for you, Corporal.'

In the end it had not been worth the bother. He had been so excited at the thought of his first real sexual encounter that it had been all over and done with in thirty seconds flat, leaving him puce-faced and panting as if he had just run a great race, stuttering a kind of apology, 'I'm sorry . . .

I'm not used—' He had never ended the sentence, for she had put her hand gently across his gaping panting mouth and he hadn't really known how to explain what he wasn't used to.

Now she washed herself modestly and slowly and somehow he sensed that she was thinking hard. Was she going to ask for money, he wondered, and didn't know how to start. My God, the alarming thought shot through his young mind, he hoped she wouldn't attempt to blackmail him by telling the Old Sweat how lousy he had been in bed! It'd be all over the battalion by nightfall, once the old sweat started spilling the beans. Christ, he wouldn't dare show his face in the NAAFI for weeks to come.

But the Jewish girl had other things on her mind than the young corporal's lack of prowess in bed. Slowly she dried the black bush with the white towel – he could see her movements quite clearly in the ceiling mirror. He could see the pensive look on her dark foreign face too. It was as if she were debating something with herself – and it was something not at all connected with his failure in bed a few minutes before.

Abruptly she turned. This time she didn't attempt to hide her skinny body from him, with the small breasts and dark triangle of hair at the loins. She crooked a finger at him. Urgently, she said (and this time her English was no longer so crude and basic as it had been before), 'Come over here. I have something to tell you. *Quick!*'

He did as he was ordered, the fact that he was exhibiting his genitals in all their nakedness to her forgotten, for there was something about her manner and tone that commanded obedience. 'What is it?'

She indicated that he should bend his head. He did so. She closed in on him. He could feel her warmth and smell her sex. He felt a sudden tingling in his loins. Was she after more? He'd heard these foreign women

10

couldn't get enough of the 'other', as the old sweat called it.

But it wasn't sex that gave this strange new urgency to the girl's manner. It was something more acute, even deadly. 'You are in danger,' she hissed into his ear.

'Danger . . . but you speak English well suddenly,' he went off at another tack.

'I'm German . . . Jewish,' she continued to whisper. 'They need me because I speak English well. But something has gone wrong. You must get out of here – at once!'

'I don't understand,' the young NCO said, totally bewildered. 'You German . . . ? They need you . . . ? Danger?' he stuttered out word after word. 'What does it mean—'

He was interrupted by the roar of a motorbike in the cobbled courtyard below and the squeal of tyres as the unknown rider braked hard. Almost immediately the sound was drowned by the tinny accordion music and rattle of the snare drums of a fast French *java* in the radio. It was as if someone wanted to cover the arrival of the motorbike.

'Is it the MPs – the military police?' the corporal cried urgently. 'We're not supposed to be here. If they catch us, they'll have my tapes off me' – he meant his corporal stripes of which he was so proud – 'in double quick time!'

Hastily she pulled aside the blackout curtain and peered out into the *cour*. She flung a glance at the two helmeted men in their leather coats and goggles sitting on the bike and its sidecar before letting the curtain slide back again. 'No, it is not the military policemen. It is her friends, the *patronne*'s. I think they have come to do you harm.' Her thin face was very pale now and, as agitated and puzzled as the young corporal was, he noted that her hands were trembling badly.

'But why are we in danger?' he persisted. 'What harm have we done? All we've been up to here in Dunkirk is to flog – er – sell some Army petrol on the black market.' He pulled a face. 'I know that's a crime and that it's bad, but that can't put us in danger, can it?'

She shook her head, obviously thinking fast now. 'No, no, not that. It is because of your . . .' she clicked her fingers impatiently as she tried to find the English word she wanted '. . . *deine Einheit . . . um Himmels willen*, what is the word?' Suddenly she had it. She started tapping her forefinger up and down and uttering sharp little sounds, as if using a morse key.

'You mean because we're in Signals?' he cried urgently.

'Yes.'

'But why?'

She didn't answer. Instead she lowered her voice even more and whispered, 'Get your friend – quick. I will show you a way out. Hurry . . . hurry.'

The corporal realized that she was close to a breakdown. She was twisting and wringing her hands alarmingly. He wasted no more time. Swiftly, he slipped on his boots and grabbed for his tunic. It wasn't there. He looked on the floor, but she didn't give him a chance to look further. 'For God's sake,' she quavered, 'go . . . find your friend. *Now!*'

Down below someone had turned up the radio even louder. The *balmusette* music seemed to make the very walls of Madame Giselle's establishment tremble. But the tinny hectic dance music seemed to lend urgency to his steps. He turned into the dimly lit corridor, while Rachel waited at the door of her own bedroom anxiously. For a moment he considered whether or not he should knock on the door of the room to which the red-haired pro had taken the Old Sweat. Then he saw the door was slightly ajar. He listened the best he could with the racket going on downstairs. The sound of the rusty bedsprings of the ancient brass bedstead was absent. The Old Sweat had finished dancing his 'mattress polka', as he called it. It should be safe to go on in. He cleared his throat in warning and pushed open the door of the fetid-smelling room.

It was empty. But as he stood there grasping the brass knob of the door, he didn't need a crystal ball to see that the room had been abandoned very hastily. The whore's red knickers were still wrapped around the bedside light, a used contraceptive lay on the floor and more importantly the Old Sweat's highly polished boots of which he was so inordinately proud – the NCO had watched him spending long evenings back at the camp 'bullshitting' their uppers with Cherry Blossom polish and a toothbrush handle till they gleamed like mirrors – had been left behind.

The corporal puffed out his cheeks in exasperation. The Old Sweat wouldn't have buggered off without his precious boots, though he knew the older man was unpredictable, especially when it came to sex and money. But where could he have gone and why had he departed so swiftly?

But he had no time to consider the problem of the Old Sweat's sudden disappearance. Abruptly the German girl was at his side, tugging at his shirt urgently. 'Come,' she hissed, 'we must go.' She brushed against him and he could feel her breasts against his chest. There was a slight stirring in his loins. He flushed and did as she commanded. With her finger held to her lips in a warning gesture to be quiet, she led him to the end of the gloomy corridor. There was a small door which he hadn't noticed before, perhaps because it was covered in the same dirty wallpaper as the rest of the corridor. He waited as she turned the rusty key in the lock. Down below the *balmusette* music had ceased abruptly, leaving behind a loud echoing silence, which somehow seemed uncanny, perhaps even a little frightening to the young NCO.

The door opened. Fetid air emerged. '*Quick!*' she ordered. He passed through into a kind of loft that stank of decay, old rotting timber and pigeon droppings. The place was pretty dark and the NCO followed close on her heels, guided here and there by patches of silver moonlight which penetrated the gaps in the old eighteenth-century slate roof. Suddenly she stopped. For a moment he thought they had come to a dead end. Down below he could hear the sound of heavy footsteps coming up the stairs. He knew instinctively they were coming for him, and perhaps the girl, too.

'*Der Schrank* – the cupboard,' she hissed. 'Help me open the door.'

Puzzled, but guessing the girl knew what she was doing, he gripped the door of the great dark old-fashioned cupboard, which in reality was a wardrobe, and tugged. The door opened with a frighteningly loud creak. The girl looked alarmed. For a moment she stood there trembling like a leaf, listening to the heavy footsteps below. But they didn't change their pace. It was obvious they hadn't heard the squeak of the wardrobe being opened.

They pushed on through the great wardrobe which covered the entrance to another loft like the one they had just left and the corporal guessed it must be that of the adjoining house. If he had had time to think, he would have told himself it was all very clever – a fine way to escape what might have been a trap. Not now, however. He was too frightened. For the girl's obvious fear was infectious and he was still bewildered by what had happened to the Old Sweat. His kind didn't scare easily, but the fact that he had disappeared leaving his prized boots behind was indicative enough of how much he had been frightened too. Something strange was going on here at this quayside knocking shop and he wanted to be no part of it. The sooner he got out of this mess the better.

A few minutes later she was leading him down the darkened steps of the house next to Madame Giselle's establishment, making him descend at the side of the steps so that the ancient boards wouldn't creak so much, hissing angrily at him every time they did so, until finally they reached the door. She hesitated and then, clicking off the dim blue light which was the stairs' sole illumination, she opened the outside door slowly, very slowly, almost as if she expected someone to be waiting for her outside.

There was no one. The blacked-out supply port appeared to have gone to sleep. The only sound was the soft lap-lap of the water on the base of the quay and further out the mournful moan of a foghorn. They might well have been the last two people left alive on the earth.

But they knew they were not. Somewhere close by there were desperate men who might well stop at nothing when the chips were down. The girl knew that much better than the young NCO, who she had just let make love to her and who soon she would never see again. She was well aware what they were capable of and that she could waste no more time if she were going to save the young Englishman's life

'Don't go to your vehicle,' she whispered, as the spectral moon disappeared behind the clouds and it became darker than ever. 'They'll be waiting for you there.'

'But I can't just go and leave government property—'

She reached up and pressed her hot hand to his mouth to stop him talking. 'Go . . . go now,' she commanded. 'Run for your life. Understood?'

He nodded and she released her hand.

'And you?' he asked hoarsely.

'Don't worry about me . . . they need me. Now – *go!*'

He went. Clinging to the shadows cast by the warehouses opposite and followed by the mournful howl of the foghorns out in the Channel, he disappeared into the darkness. Hurriedly the girl closed the door behind him and started back, her mind full of what she had to do now – and soon – before it was too late.

At the top of the street, the two Flemings waited, the silencers already attached to their big German Luger pistols . . .

PART ONE:
A PIANIST IS CAPTURED

One

'Nothing doing yet,' the old lady with the shabby cardboard suitcase was saying. 'Looks to me as if Hitler will never move.'

'Ay,' the big Scottish woman in the shawl and bonnet sitting next to her on the bench in front of the penny chocolate machine agreed, 'looks like another bluidy Hundred Years' War to me, ye ken.'

. But if Hitler wasn't moving, Edinburgh's Waverly station was. Drafts of troops from every Scottish regiment – the Hell's Last Issue, the Pontius Pilate's Bodyguard – and the rest were staggering down the platforms weighed down like pack mules with their equipment; officious-looking Railway Transport Officers, all armed with the inevitable clipboard and pencil, were ticking off names and trains, shouting orders through their megaphones; middle class, good ladies from the Women's Voluntary Service were handing out tea and sympathy to the leaving men, lovers sobbed in a last embrace as the train whistles and the guards' commands summoned them to a final parting; and everywhere, there were the hard-faced redcaps, the military policemen, eyes invisible under the slanting peaks of their caps, searching for malefactors and deserters.

Waverley station this late May afternoon was a typical wartime station, a place full of expectations, potential adventure and sadness. And, Staff Sergeant Mackenzie, formerly of Heidelberg and Oxford universities, Cambridge

Fellow of Comparative Indo-European Philology couldn't help thinking, possibly sudden violent death.

Not that his face, as he slumped there with his kit on the bench, dressed in the ill-fitting uniform of a private soldier in the King's Own Scottish Borderers, bored with his reading matter – a battered copy of the *Lilliput* – revealed any such deep thoughts. Instead his features had assumed that aspect common to all private soldiers in this period of the 'Phoney War' of 1940: bovine acceptance of his humble lot, though if he could afford a couple of wee drams (which he patently couldn't), he might well break into that well known chant of bored licentious soldiery: '*Why are we waiting, oh why are we waiting?*' accompanied by the ritual 'ba-baing' that was calculated to turn sergeant-majors a puce colour and bring them to the fringe of a heart attack with suppressed rage.

He had been sitting there now for an hour or more and it seemed that the middle-aged porter, who looked more like a retired boxer than a wielder and pusher of the LMS trolleys he pushed to and fro, had taken pity on the lone KOSB. More than once he had ambled across to the soldier and had offered him a Woodbine. Once had stood guard over the soldier's kit as he had gone over to the Salvation Army canteen. 'A wee dram'd be better, laddie,' the porter had exclaimed, 'but I fear ye'll have to make do with yon Sally Ann tay.'

Now as the crowds began to thicken again, though the fact didn't seem to alter the middle-aged porter's work routine – slow and very slow – the latter crossed to the lone soldier yet again. On the opposite platform a trainload of Jocks for the 51st Highland Division had just pulled in and the young reinforcements, mostly drunk, were loudly bawling, '*There's jam, jam mixed up with the ham in the quartermaster's store . . . My eyes are dim, I cannot see, I haena got my specs wi' me . . .*'

The porter grinned good-heartedly and said, 'They'll soon knock the piss an' vinegar outa them once they get them to France.' His accent was broad Scots, but when he bent and whispered to the KOSB, it had changed to that of a middle-class Englishman. 'They're coming in from Buckie, sir, to catch the London train . . . in fifteen minutes.'

The KOSB private didn't raise his head, but when he answered his voice was sharp and authorative. 'Everyone in place, Inspector?'

'Yessir. I've got a man in the left luggage office over there. There's another up with the ladies of the Women's Voluntary Service and I've got another up on Princes Street – on the steps – just in case they try to make a run for it. They're all armed and alerted now.'

'Good work, Inspector,' the KOSB answered sotto voce, accepting yet another of the middle-aged 'porter's' precious Woodbines. 'Look out for the ends of their trousers. They might well be stained with sea salt.'

'They waded ashore, sir?'

'We think so. The dinghy was found far out at sea. Perhaps they couldn't make it over the breakers.'

'Thank you, sir, for the tip.' The porter straightened up. 'Don't worry, sir. We'll capture the Hun swine. My lads are very keen.'

'Fine, Inspector,' the KOSB answered. 'But remember, they're probably armed and we want to take them alive.'

'I'll remember, sir.' Suddenly the porter reverted to the broad Scots he had assumed for this trap, saying, 'Wiel, I'll be awa' the nu.'

Staff Sergeant Mackenzie, well trained in phonetics by the celebrated Dr Jones who had invented the International Phonetics Code, allowed himself a small grin. The inspector-cum-porter was trying hard, but somehow he didn't think his assumed accent would stand up to professional scrutiny. Then he dismissed the porter, who was now directing some lost squaddies (probably *misdirecting* them would be a better

21

description), and concentrated on the immediate problem at hand.

At the moment, Old Jerry seemed to be going all out trying to infiltrate spies into the UK. Ever since the Germans had taken Norway a month or so ago, they had been using their new base at Stavanger to start agents across the poorly patrolled North Sea into Scotland and land them at suitably remote spots. Twice the RAF had shot down German flying boats with civilians, equipped with the tools of their trade, aboard. Unfortunate in both cases that the Luftwaffe crews and their agent passengers had bought it, so he and his boss Captain Dalby had had no chance to find out what exactly this influx of spies into Britain was intended for. Then, as his chief, a veteran of the 'Old War' as he called it, had remarked thoughtfully, 'The Hun's up to something, sergeant. You'd think they'd make their main effort in France with our BEF*. But no, England seems to be the main objective. The question is – *why?*'

Now, ever since a Scottish herring trawler had spotted the strange vessel flying the Norwegian flag off the fog-bound coast of Iceland, with a bearing on Northern Scotland, followed a day later by the coastguard finding the abandoned dinghy, he and his chief had been anxiously waiting for the action. Now it seemed to Mackenzie that it was about to commence.

Early that morning two men with suitcases had walked into Blackpool railway station east of Scotland's Portgordon and had purchased tickets to Edinburgh. The ticket collector and the ticket clerk had been a little suspicious, but then in that part of Scotland strangers were always suspect and they had dismissed them.

It was only when Angus Dunphie, a small boy who was, according to the locals, spy mad, had pointed out to the ticket

*British Expeditionary Force

22

collector, waving his *Wizard* at the man as if he might hit him with the comic if he didn't do something, 'Yon strangers have got wet breeks', that something was done.

There had been no rain that morning, so how come the travellers, both with heavy suitcases, wore trousers soaked to the knee? Had they been in the sea?

Now, Staff Sergeant Mackenzie suspected they had and that these were other German agents being smuggled into the country to carry out some task, which had to be so important to the German Secret Service, the *Abwehr*, that seemingly the whole of *Abwehr*'s Hamburg branch was solely concerned with this, as yet, unknown objective.

Now the trap was set, he told himself, all they needed was for the two victims to walk into it and be captured. For it was vital that the agents, if such they were, were taken alive. Once they were safely locked away in Camp 020 at Ham, south-east of London, old Colonel 'Tin Eye' Stephens, the camp's commandant, would soon have them singing like a bird. His staff, all of them hard men themselves, said of their chief (behind his back), 'Old Tin Eye can make a ruddy mummy talk!'

Mackenzie sat there, suddenly miles away from the task ahead. Only half a year before, he had been adding to his Cambridge D.Phil. the German equivalent at Hamburg University. In that beautiful northern city set on the banks of its internal lakes, the Outer and Inner Alster, he had been happy. Hamburg had always been 'red'; the locals had never taken to the Nazis. Indeed its citizens had been very pro-British and aped British ways, even dress. Didn't the locals say that when it rained in England, the Hamburgers unfurled their umbrellas? Yet despite all that, he knew ever since he had become a member of Captain Dalby's Secret Field Intelligence Police that all the while in that same city, not a hundred yards away from the university where he had studied, the German *Abwehr* had already been plotting

Britain's downfall. Even then they had been slipping agents into Britain by the score. It was a terrible kind of duplicity, and in a way when he had found out he had felt a kind of betrayal. Hell's bells, he had been considering asking one of his fellow students, Helga Ramussen, to marry him once he had been officially appointed to a post in Cambridge.

Now he asked himself whether he should hate those Germans he had drunk with and made love to. But before he could dwell on that overwhelming question, the boom of the loudspeaker further down the platform alerted him to the fact that the time for action had come. 'The train now approaching platform one,' the distorted metallic voice announced, 'is the nine o'clock slow train from . . .'

He listened no more. Instinctively his hand reached in the pocket of his greatcoat where he had hidden his .38. Opposite, the porter had dropped his cigarette and was stubbing it out busily. At the left luggage office, another of the inspector's men withdrew his head hastily from the open counter. Abruptly all was haste and nervous anticipation. Mackenzie could feel a vein at his temple begin to throb urgently and his breath started to come in short sharp gasps. The adrenalin was flowing. He and the rest were ready for action . . .

Slowly, with a clatter of pistons, the hiss of steam escaping, the furious clank of wheels being brought to a halt, the slow country train began to stop.

Everywhere doors were flung open. Soldiers started to descend, heavy steel-shod ammunition boots stamping on the platform, as helpful civilians passed them their kitbags and packs. Women passed babies – most of them shrieking – through the windows to other helpful civilians. In the sole first class carriage, a haughty-looking woman in Highland tweeds and a pork-pie hat leaned out and cried in a very English voice, 'I say, porter, over here, will you?'

24

Studiously the porter avoided her gaze, instinctively letting go of his barrow. He, like the rest of them, had his gaze fixed hypnotically on the emerging passengers looking for the two civilians with the wet lower trousers; they mustn't escape the trap.

Mackenzie did the same. But he looked, too, for the cut of the suspects' suits, for he knew what the Germans called the *Englische Mode* was totally off the mark. Like all continentals, the Germans inclined to too tight a waist and too bold a check; normally he could spot a German by his suit a mile off.

But this May day he seemed to be out of luck. All the males coming off the train seemed to be quite normally dressed and already the crowd was beginning to thin out. Out of the corner of his eye, he could see the inspector's face had dropped too, as he obviously started to wonder if they'd missed the two alleged agents.

Then suddenly he had them. Two men had got off the same carriage, both carrying large suitcases. It appeared they were about to go their separate ways. But before they did, they did something that seemed to be untypical. They put their cases on the platform and shook hands. Mackenzie told himself that this could naturally be old-fashioned British politeness, though it was not customary for people who travelled third class as these men had done to engage in such courtesies. Then they bowed stiffly from the waist. He gave a little gasp. It was them! Britons didn't bow to each other on parting. Suddenly he felt the hand gripping the .38 revolver in the pocket of his greatcoat go wet with sweat. *He had the buggers!*

He wasted no further time. Swiftly he gestured at the inspector, pointing to the two men who had now separated and were walking up the platform a few yards from each other. The inspector nodded back his understanding. He gave a hand signal to his men. Then he, too, followed Mackenzie up the platform, pushing his way past the ticket collector at the barrier with a curt nod and the flash of his police ID.

Mackenzie came close to the first of the two men. Now he could see the dirty white salt marks on the man's trousers, though he had obviously got rid of the stains on his shoes. He was the man they were looking for, all right. He stopped and waited for the man, who was dark-featured and had a hooked nose which lent a certain Oriental look about him.

Mackenzie decided he'd make the approach, one that was as calming as possible. He didn't want the man to panic. '*Guten Tag*,' he began quietly in German, '*darf ich Ihre Papiere seh—*'

He got no further. The man reacted with surprising speed. He jerked the heavy suitcase forward and struck Mackenzie directly on the shins. The latter gasped with pain and shock. The next moment the man was running towards the barrier, ignoring the curses and cries of the other passengers as he weaved his way through, pushing and pulling in his desperate need to escape.

'Stop him!' Mackenzie yelled, straightening up and trying to locate the other man, who'd obviously be alerted by now.

Behind him the inspector spread his arms like kids do at playtime in the schoolyard when they try to stop their classmates. But the running man, face glazed with sweat, eyes like a man demented, was no school kid. He gave the inspector a shove so that he staggered back against the iron barrier. The ticket collector shot out his right foot; the man sprang over it easily. He was almost through now. In a minute he'd disappear up the steps which led to Princess Street and that would be fatal.

The inspector obviously thought so, too. He pulled out his big service revolver. 'Stop,' he yelled. 'In the name of the law!'

At any other time, Mackenzie would have laughed at the policeman's use of the ancient formula. Not now. Everything was going wrong. Now the inspector was going to shoot and if he hit the running man . . .

Mackenzie hadn't time to think that thought to an end. In the same instant that the running man started to vault the barrier, the inspector fired. The man shrieked. He seemed to be suspended in mid-air for an eternity, arms flailing wildly as he attempted to keep to his balance. Next instant he fell backwards and lay dead or unconscious on the cold concrete, the blood already beginning to form a dark-red pool around his inert body.

Two

'You Hun swine,' the voice bellowed from down below where the prisoners' huts were. 'I'll have the Hun hide off'n you, if you don't smarten your ideas up. *Himmel, Arsch und Wolkenbruch, los!*'

Mackenzie grinned and said to the now newly promoted Major Dalby, 'Colonel Stephens is on good form, sir,'

A little wearily his chief shared his grin. Mackenzie could see he had been drinking. Perhaps it was stress, worry, even the pain in his legs from the wounds he had suffered on the Somme back in July 1916 in the Old War. Still, the young NCO thought the 'old man' was taking in too much whisky these days.

'Yes, Mac,' Dalby agreed, 'he is. Somehow he gets away with it. God knows what the Swiss Red Cross wallahs would say if they caught him banging away at prisoners like that.'

Mackenzie nodded and told himself that the Swiss Red Cross, those supposed neutrals, who were supplying Germany with a hell of a lot of their war supplies, would have a devil of a job finding and entering Camp 020. Old Tin Eye Stephens would see to that. He cleared his throat and Dalby returned the silver flask from which he had been drinking to the pocket of his somewhat shabby service dress.

'All right,' Dalby said, 'fill me in, Mac, if you would.'

'The first chap, Meier, died on us unfortunately before we could get him into dock in Edinburgh.'

Dalby shrugged carelessly. It was as if he had long given up caring whether people died or lived. Perhaps he was right in his attitude, Mackenzie told himself, though it was hard for a young man like himself to understand. Still the Old Man had seen a lot of violent deaths in his time and undoubtedly he'd see more before this war was over. 'The second – Krueger by name, sir – pulled a knife on me. But I . . .' He shrugged and didn't continue save to add, 'He's here now.'

Dalby gave his subordinate a weary smile. 'Good show, Mac. That's the stuff to give the troops. Has Tin Eye got anything out of him yet, d'you know? This whole business here in the UK is very puzzling. I think it's making me turn to drink, Mac.' He laughed, but there was no pleasure to the sound; his statement was all too true.

Mackenzie didn't comment. Instead he said, 'Colonel Stevens plays with his cards close to his chest, sir, as you know. But I'm sure he'll have got something out of Krueger. But this we already know from the examination of his and the dead man's suitcase, they were both agents. Both packed guns, had secret inks, the usual stuff. Krueger had this.' He handed the piece of cardboard, covered with letters and black cramped handwriting in the spiky German style.

Dalby took out his glasses and focused on the piece of cardboard. He read out the first batch of letters, 'Q . . . M . . . X.' He then translated the German text which went with them: 'Wait until . . . Q . . . R . . . M . . . *Störsender* . . . disturbance in Sending.' He looked up and took off the glasses. 'Excellent, Mac,' he exclaimed. 'So he's a pianist, our German friend, eh?'

'Exactly, sir.'

Dalby looked thoughtful for a few moments. Outside Tin Eye Stevens was shouting in English at presumably one of his subordinates. 'You must be motivated by an implacable hatred of the enemy. There's going be none of this "poor old

29

Jerry, bad luck old fellow for being caught . . ." No, sir, not in Camp 020!' He warmed to his theme: 'No chivalry. No chat. No cigarettes. Figuratively, a spy in wartime should be always held at the point of a bloody bayonet!'

Mackenzie told himself what a bloodthirsty bugger the monocled prison camp commander was. If anyone was going to get anything out of Krueger, it would be Tin Eye.

Dalby spoke slowly and reflectively. 'So if this Krueger chap is a pianist, a radio operator, he was scheduled to work for someone else. Do you think the dead man – er, Meier – was to be the man he was to work for?'

Mackenzie shook his head. 'No sir. Very definitely not, sir. Meier had a mission of his own. To spy out airfields in south-west England. We found a list of their locations on him. It was then to be his mission to get back to the continent with whatever information he found out as soon as possible.'

'That's interesting,' Dalby commented, as if to himself. 'Carry on.'

'He was to memorize the material, take no notes or anything. Everything had to be in his head so—'

'He wouldn't need a pianist.' Dalby beat the young NCO to it.

'Yessir.'

'So that means one thing, Mac, doesn't it?'

'What, sir?'

Dalby was suddenly pleased with himself for some reason known only to himself. For a moment or so it caused him to tease the younger man. 'Well, you're the chap with all those degrees and brains, you should be able to tumble what it means quicker than a poor old addle-brained crock like yours truly.'

'I'm out of my depth, sir,' Mackenzie retorted. He wasn't offended by the teasing; he was glad to see the chief happy for once.

'Then I'll tell you, Mac.' Suddenly Dalby was his usual grim-faced self again, brow furrowed in a worried look. 'Krueger was intended to be the pianist for someone else. In other words, there is some German agent of importance still loose in the country when we thought we'd rounded them all up back in Autumn '39. Now it's our task, an urgent task, I must emphasize, Mac, to find this unknown . . . er . . . agent. Why, you might ask?'

Mackenzie waited, wondering if the old man was taking this matter too seriously.

'I shall tell you,' Dalby continued. 'Because I think there's more to this, Mac, than meets the eye. Why waste agents on this country? The Huns surely have enough to do using their *Abwehr* blokes to find out our dispositions in France. That's where the active front will be when the Boche finally decide to come out and fight, which they will undoubtedly do. After all, Mac, we know what they're capable of. We experienced that in Venlo last November*. They'll stop at nothing.'

'Understood, sir, so we want Krueger to lead us to this unknown agent toot sweet. But Krueger looks a hard bastard to me. I don't think he's going to crack so soon. Even Colonel Stevens—'

'Someone taking my name in vain?'

The two of them turned a little startled and clicked to attention. It was Tin Eye himself, his voice as usual booming as he ordered, 'Stand easy.' They did so and he scrutinized them through the monocle he affected, saying, 'You've come about that Hun Krueger no doubt.'

Dalby nodded.

'Tight as a drum, the German bugger,' Tin Eye said. 'Nazi through and through, but you must give him his due, he's a loyal swine. But I think, gentlemen, we might get something

*See Leo Kessler: *Murder at Colditz* (Severn House) for further details.

out of him yet. I think –' he stroked his somewhat gross face thoughtfully – 'I'll sentence him to cell 14, if he doesn't spill the beans.'

'Cell 14!' Dalby snapped. 'I won't be party to any torture.'

Tin Eye laughed. 'You don't need to be. Cell 14 doesn't exist, but the prisoners think it does. Sentence a Hun to cell 14 and he thinks he's going to be subjected to indescribable torture. Usually he starts singing like a yellow canary then. Now,' he was businesslike again, 'what do you want to know from this Krueger fellah, eh?'

'This Meier,' Dalby said as outside the air-raid sirens started sounding their thin mournful wail. 'Where he was going?'

He nodded to Mackenzie, who jumped in hastily with: 'He had a ticket from Waverley, Edinburgh to London King's Cross. Thereafter we don't know who his contact was going to be. You see, he was meeting some other Jerry, we're sure of that. After all he was not an active agent, but merely a pianist, who was to transmit for someone who was doing the actual spying.'

'Got it.' Despite his somewhat gross appearance, Tin Eye was quick on the uptake. Mackenzie knew, too, that the camp commandant spoke several languages fluently. He wasn't the bully, loud-mouthed and coarse, that he made himself out to be. That was probably part of the image that he cultivated in order to intimidate his 'charges', as he called them. 'All right then, let's get to the interrogation room and wheel the bugger in.'

Outside, the wail of the sirens sounding the alert were coming ever closer. But none of the three seemed to notice; they were so intent on solving the mystery of Krueger's contact man.

Tin Eye seated himself at the head of the highly polished

table. Dalby and Mackenzie sat on either side of him on the stiff upright chairs. 'You'll be with me on the tribunal,' Tin Eye explained. 'I always make these things very precise and formal. The Huns think they're actually being tried by some kind of secret court.'

Now, with Tin Eye dressed in his best uniform, chest ablaze with medal ribbons so that Dalby and Mackenzie felt decidedly shabby in his presence, he snapped at the redcap at the door, 'All right, prisoner in, sergeant!'

'Sir!' The military policeman turned, opened the door and cried, 'All right, bring up the prisoner.'

Someone shouted a command in German. There was the stamp of heavy boots in the corridor outside. Next moment two MPs, both armed with revolvers, swung round the door pushing Krueger in front of them.

The German agent looked paler and thinner than when Mackenzie had last seen him and his drawn face showed he was afraid – but then Mackenzie himself was a little awed by the stiff cold formality of the tribunal – yet at the same time, Krueger still seemed determined. Mackenzie sensed he'd still be a tough nut to crack.

Tin Eye wasted no time. He read out the prisoner's details swiftly and then bellowed in German, 'We know all about you, Krueger. You are a German spy. You have been captured out of German uniform inside British territory. The penalty for that is, as you know, *death.*'

He let his words sink in, glaring at Krueger all the time through that monocle which had given him his nickname, and then said, 'The doctor here –' he indicated Dalby, who showed no apparent surprise that he had suddenly become a medical man – 'has asked me to mitigate your sentence. He maintains that you and your dead comrade were just pawns in a nasty underhand game, which we knew all about right from the start before you even landed on the Scottish coast.'

Mackenzie thought he caught a glimmer of surprise at that revelation on Krueger's face. If there was, Tin Eye didn't give the prisoner a chance to express it.

Instead, he went on rapidly, 'Now, Krueger, I ask you why should I accord with the doctor's wishes and allow you to escape the death penalty? You have given us no co-operation since you have been in Camp 020. You have been stubborn about the odd really unimportant detail we have asked you to give us, hasn't he, Police Commisioner?' Tin Eye turned to Mackenzie who was surprised to find that, although his arm bore the crown and three stripes of a staff sergeant and he was wearing the khaki uniform of the British Army, he had abruptly become a senior member of the police force. Still he managed to stutter 'Yes', and add in German, '*Wer ist Ihr Kontaktperson in England . . . und wo?*'

Krueger looked uneasy. It was clear his surroundings and all these questions being fired at him in fluent German were upsetting him. He had always regarded the English as a reserved, rather stupid people, who hid their stupidity behind a kind of aristocratic arrogance. Here, he was finding out that the English were not at all stupid; indeed they were tougher and more threatening than the Gestapo officials who had vetted him before he had been accepted by the *Abwehr*. In Germany at least they would have given him some kind of secret trial before they sentenced him to death for spying. Here, on the contrary, he had already been apparently sentenced to death in his absence. His resolution began to waver. At least the doctor, the oldest of the tribunal, had spoken out in his favour. Should he tell them what he knew in the hope that he might save his life? Would they honour any promise they might give him now if he revealed his knowledge?

Outside, the flak was beginning to thunder in the distance and from their vantage point in the upper storey where the tribunal was held they could see one of the barrage balloons going down in flames, trailing smoke behind it like a wounded and suddenly deflated elephant.

Krueger licked his suddenly parched lips. On the opposite side of the great table, the three of them waited. Outside, despite the thunder of the ack-ack cannon, they could hear the sinister drone of a lone aircraft. Even without seeing it, they knew instinctively it was German; and to Mackenzie, it almost seemed as if the enemy plane was searching for Camp 020. He told himself he was being fanciful, yet he could not dismiss the thought. It was as if the plane were risking being shot down by going so slow in order to find a specific objective.

'Well?' Tin Eye broke the silence with a throaty growl. His hand reached for the officer swagger stick which lay on the table in front of him.

The prisoner construed the gesture to mean that in a minute the camp commandant was about to strike him with it. It was, of course, what Tin Eye intended him to think.

Krueger's bottom lip quavered and he said in a low voice, '*Douvre . . . sie wohnt in Douvre.*'

'What did he say, Major?' Tin Eye demanded of Dalby. 'Couldn't hear the bugger with all this bloody racket.'

Dalby shook his head and flashed a look at Mackenzie, the youngest of the three-man tribunal. But before the latter could say what he thought he had just heard, the whoosh and roar of a bomb slamming into the building threw him out of his chair and smashed him into the opposite wall. Next moment the roof came slithering down in a brick avalanche filling the room with dust and obscuring the sudden moans and screams of the wounded and the trapped. Sprawled out against the wall, feeling very sick, Mackenzie shook his head and tried to clear the black fog which was threatening to overcome him. To no avail. His eyes rolled upwards and he was out.

High above, the lone Junkers 88 did one more turn and

took the photos as ordered by Berlin, then the pilot had had enough. '*Los Jungs!*' he cried, as the brown cotton balls of smoke, which were the flak, came hurtling up once more. '*Hauen wir ab . . . Dalli . . . dalli*'

His men needed no urging. 'Father Christmas' had promised them the Iron Cross First Class, if they carried out this mission successfully, plus a three-day leave in Berlin. Now they wanted to live to enjoy those rewards, especially in view of what they knew was soon to come. The senior pilot jerked his stick back hard. The Junkers rose like a bird. A moment later they were through the cloud base, and below the firing ceased. They had done it.

Three

G reat Crap on the Christmas tree! the elegant naval aide cursed to himself, Old 'Father Christmas' seemed to be as damned dizzy and sloppy as ever. Didn't he realize he was going to meet Grand Admiral Raeder in five minutes and then perhaps the Führer himself? Why, the little admiral with his benign expression and mop of snowy-white hair, which had given him his nickname, looked like a shitting scarecrow. He'd even bought his pet twin dachshunds with him. How could a sloppy old man who adored poodles be taken seriously as the head of the *Abwehr* when he looked such a mess?

Admiral Canaris, nicknamed Father Christmas, turned from looking at himself in the big mirror in the corridor which led to the conference room. 'How do I look, Dietz?' he asked, beaming at the elegant aide in his smart, blue naval uniform. While he spoke, one of the dachshunds lifted his rear leg and urinated over the admiral's shoe. He didn't seem to notice.

'Excellent, sir,' the aide replied dutifully. 'But may I suggest you transfer your Iron Cross to the other breast, sir. You've got it on the wrong side of your tunic.'

The admiral looked and said in his usual mild tone, 'I say, you're right. Perhaps you would be so kind as to rectify the matter for me?'

'Sir.' Hastily he fumbled with the admiral's shabby tunic, which obviously hadn't been cleaned for a long time. All the same, he noticed Father Christmas smelled strongly of some high quality eau de cologne. Perhaps it was to hide the smell, he told himself.

As he did so, the great doors at the end of the corridor opened and a giant SS officer, clad in black with white cross-straps, slammed his boots down on the floor, as if he were back at the SS barracks in Berlin-Lichtefelde, and bellowed, 'The Grand Admiral requests you enter . . . The Führer is delayed.' He frowned suspiciously as the suddenly red-faced aide withdrew his hand hastily from inside the admiral's tunic. Dietz knew all about the rumours that old Father Christmas was a secret 'warm brother'. Berlin was full of malicious rumours about his relationship with his African servant Mohammed. He didn't care, but he didn't want to be associated with anything like that. A man could get his head chopped off very smartly for being a 'warm brother' in the Third Reich these days.

'Thank you. You are most kind,' the admiral said and smiled. 'I say, would you mind looking after the dogs. The Grand Admiral – well you understand, Dietz.'

Dietz did. Grand Admiral Raeder was old school. He'd have a heart attack if Canaris went into a conference holding the leash of the two dogs, which seemed to piss all the time. 'No, sir,' he said and a little unhappily he took over the dogs, while the giant SS officer stared at him, as if he felt that Dietz might blow him a kiss at any momeent.

Raeder looked exactly what he was – a stuffy elderly officer who still lived in the age of the German Imperial Navy in which he had once served so proudly. He even wore the old-fashioned raised stiff collar, which his younger officers called 'a father murderer' because of its strangulating tightness. He looked up from his maps and muttered, 'Morning, Canaris.'

'Morning, *Herr Grossadmiral.*'

'Well, you know why we're here, Canaris,' Raeder said

and looked at Canaris's shoes as if wondering why they appeared to be soaked.

'The Führer has made his final decision then, Grand Admiral?'

'*Jawohl, wir marschieren!*'

'The date?' Suddenly Canaris's sallow lazy features, which indicated that he had other more exotic blood running in his veins than that of the ordinary German, were animated by a keen, even cunning, look.

'Friday, 10th May.'

Canaris nodded as he absorbed the information. 'That gives me another five days to finalize the operation.'

Raeder looked puzzled. 'What operation, Canaris? I don't know of any separate *Abwehr* operation, save for a few minor missions on our western frontier, within the general plan for the great offensive.' His wooden, stupid, old man's face looked almost angry now, as if he felt Canaris had been going behind his back to curry favour with the Führer. For it was well known that Hitler liked the head of the Secret Service and felt he was a lot smarter than many of his general staff officers.

'Part of the plan to finish off the Tommies, Grand Admiral,' Canaris replied in that silken subdued tone he often used when he felt he had surprised his colleagues: one that often irritated them beyond measure, as well. 'It is clear, at least to me, that the French have lost the will to fight. All my agents in that unfortunate country tell me that. Can you expect sacrifices from a country that is concerned with *foie gras* and two hundred varieties of cheese?' He giggled, an oddly feminine sound, which upset Raeder. But he didn't comment; he let Canaris continue.

'The English, Grand Admiral, are different. They might not be very bright, but they are a stubborn people. They will keep on fighting. So if we, as the Führer wishes, are to have a quick peace in Europe, we must see the Tommies off very quickly. And I and my people are to play a modest part in ensuring that the English flee *our* Europe and return to their rainswept cold little island and drink their tea to their hearts' content.'

Raeder had had enough. Canaris was too clever, he told himself angrily, he needed to be cut down to size. 'And pray, how do you propose to do that, my dear Admiral?' he asked haughtily. 'After all, you do not possess an army, not even a single battleship.'

'How?' Canaris echoed, not losing that mocking supercilious smile of his, which Raeder found so irritating. 'Why, sir, with a bunch of whores . . .'

On that same day on the other side of the continent, Mackenzie completed his daily visit to the wounded from that strange lone plane attack on Camp 020, and for the first time sat down to examine the problem on hand: the location of the German spy to whom Krueger had intended to report as his 'pianist'; though that particular pianist would never play his radio 'piano' again. The bomb had severed his hands, one at the wrist, the other at the lower arm. Krueger would survive, the quacks at the London Military Hospital maintained. But he was so deeply in shock due to his severe injuries that they forbad any further interrogation for a while.

Tin Eye, whose pride had been injured worse than his wounded leg, had snorted angrily, rising from his hospital cot with rage. 'Who cares if the Hun bugger lives or dies – he's going to the gallows as it is. Now's the time to get it out of him when he's so low. Just let me get at him.'

Tin Eye had been forcibly restrained by two big nurses and the medical brigadier had been summoned in the end to warn the commandant of 020: 'That if you don't behave yourself, Colonel, I shall be forced to restrain you – in a straitjacket.' That did it: Tin Eye remained quiet; he had met his match at last.

Now, twenty-four hectic hours after the attack, Mackenzie sat in the office trying to marshal the few facts they already knew and make some sense of them. But even the arranging of the facts, which for a trained researcher as he had been up until recently should have been as easy as falling off a log, was difficult. Always at the back of his mind, he was nagged by the mystery of that lone Junkers which had definitely had Camp 020 as its objective. But why?

Wishing he dare enter the major's room and mix himself a swift drink of Dalby's whisky, but resisting the temptation, he forced himself by sheer naked will power to try to fit the jigsaw together.

In the prisoner's last statement before that strange bombing attack had commenced, he had said something about *Douvre*. That was where the agent was supposed to be located, and if his ears hadn't deceived him Krueger had said 'she'. But perhaps he hadn't heard the prisoner correctly. Stick to this 'Douvre', he ordered himself. That you definitely heard.

For a few minutes, while outside the sentries paced back and forth along the gravel path, occasionally contravening King's Regulations by whispering to each other as they passed with 'Roll on death and we can have a go at the frigging angels' or 'Me plates o' meat ain't half killing me . . . and I'm excused boots, too . . . got a chitty from the MO', he ran his mind over English towns beginning with D. There was Deal, Daventry, Doncaster, Donington . . . But for the life of him he couldn't think of one called Douvre. Then suddenly it came to him with the startling suddenness of a revelation: Dover. *Douvre was the French version of 'Dover*!

'Christmas Almighty,' he yelled to no one in particular. 'Of course.'

The Krueger bloke had been in France some time or other –
at that moment Mackenzie didn't ask himself why a German
spy had been in an allied country recently. There, he had
picked up the French name for Dover. So far so good. But
Mackenzie went on to ask himself why would the Germans
plant a spy in Dover? The Kentish port was naturally used
for transporting troops to the BEF and for the destroyer
squadrons which patrolled the Channel. But, as a source
of intelligence-gathering for the Jerries, he couldn't think
of it as being highly important. London or one of the great
Midland industrial cities, such as Birmingham or Coventry
where they made the British Army's weapons of war, were
surely more important.

Mackenzie sucked his teeth as he pondered the problem.
Outside they were changing the sentries now, using the
century-old drill patterns and orders, as if this was peacetime
and Britain was not engaged in total war. 'Old Guard,' the
sergeant-of-the-guard was bellowing, 'Will turn about –
about – turn!' The heavy boots stamped on the gravel with
the harsh precision of peacetime soldiering. 'New guard –
take up duties!' There was another stamp of boots hitting
the gravel, as if they fully intended to make a hole in it and
then there was silence again.

When he looked back at that moment in the long years to
come, Mackenzie thought it marked a change. He wasn't a
fanciful man, but that old-fashioned military ceremony, the
last one he would witness, seemed to him to signify the end
of Old England and its Victorian confidence that its great
Empire – all that red on the map – would always triumph,
come what may. In its place there would be a surly, sullen
feeling of malaise, as if the world had played a dirty trick
on the English and their century-old achievements.

Mackenzie frowned and told himself that the events of
the last twenty-four hours had set his mind and imagination
off racing at top speed. He'd better restrain himself and

concentrate on the problem at hand. Why Dover? Again he had come back to that overwhelming question.

Was there some connection with Dover being the main supply port for the BEF and the fact that Krueger had used the French name for the place, as if he had been in the country previously? Was there a link between Dover and France that made the port important enough for the *Abwehr* to have an agent there and send him a pianist? More significantly: was the little network being set up in Dover – and he knew it was not yet operating; it couldn't without a pianist – of such great importance that the Germans would send a lone bomber to attempt to kill Krueger?

For that was how he had now interpreted the attack. Why risk just one plane in an attack, which might have been supposed to have been launched against London: one single plane facing the whole might of the capital's anti-aircraft defences? There would have been no point in such a raid. Mackenzie reasoned that the Junkers' attack had been a deliberately, carefully planned one on Camp 020, where in the light of recent events, there could be only one important prisoner – Krueger!

Mackenzie puffed out his cheeks in exasperation and frustration, too. It followed, therefore, that the set-up in Dover, whatever it was, was so important that the *Abwehr*, together with the German Air Force, would go to such lengths to kill Krueger before he could spill the beans. 'But Christ bloody Almighty, what is it?' he cried out loud.

It was then that Major Dalby came in, arm still in a sling. 'Morning, Mac,' he said, his face grey from the pain of his shoulder wound.

Hastily Mackenzie scrambled to his feet to stand to attention. 'Morning, sir,' he snapped.

Dalby forced a grin and nodded that Mackenzie should sit down. 'You'll never make a real soldier in a month of Sundays, Mac, so relax.' He took off his cap and pulled the silver whisky flask out of his tunic pocket. It was still not midday, but that didn't worry the major. He had the old front-line soldier's habit of drinking at all times of the day. He gasped and said, 'That hits the spot.' He sat down, looked idly at the papers on his desk, tossed them in the OUT tray and said, 'Bad news.'

'What, sir?'

Dalby answered without any apparent emotion. 'That Hun bugger Krueger gone and snuffed it on us,' he grunted. 'Well, that's put the kybosh on that line of enquiry, hasn't it just.'

Mackenzie nodded his agreement and waited.

After a minute's silence, Dalby said, 'What now, brown cow?'

'Hmm,' Mackenzie sighed and then said, 'We could start at Dover, sir?'

'And do what? We already know that radio detection has picked up nothing from there, even from an amateur pianist waiting for the professional, the late unlamented Herr Krueger, to appear.'

'Perhaps,' Mackenzie suggested, 'the man in place might be using some sort of human transport to get his messages across to France and then on to Germany?'

'How do you mean?'

'Well, sir, there is constant ship traffic between Dover and Calais and Dunkirk. Supplies for the troops, reinforcements for the BEF and the like, and the seamen manning those ships are not all British. There'll be Frenchmen and perhaps other nationalities, too. They'd be open to a bribe for smuggling messages across.'

'I wouldn't put anything past the Froggies. Sell their own mothers for a few sou,' Dalby grunted.

There was a moment's silence till Dalby roused himself, seemingly with an effort, to say, 'All right, Mac. Let's go have a dekko.'

'Dekko at what, sir?'

44

'Dover, of course. Get on the blower to the head of the local Field Security, tell him we're coming and that he is to have anything relevant ready for us. Then we'll have a wander round ourselves.' He pulled out his handkerchief and mopped his brow, as if it were hot, though their office was really quite cool. 'Bit of fresh sea air won't do us any harm, don't suppose.'

'Yessir,' Mackenzie answered. 'I'll get right on to it.'

'Good man.' Dalby mopped his brow again with his large khaki-coloured handkerchief. 'Funny time . . . funny weather, eh? Something in the wind somewhere and it ain't the ozone.'

As Mackenzie bent over the office safe to take out the secret telephone book detailing all Intelligence numbers throughout the kingdom, he nodded his agreement. The chief was right. There was something in the wind and it wasn't ozone.

And five hundred miles away, Adolf Hitler, his face glazed with sweat, eyes bulging like those of a man demented, brought his speech to the admirals to an end with a fiery tirade: 'We shall bring England to her knees. Once our attack in France is successful, the English will have to surrender. We shall first break the English Army in France. More importantly we shall then destroy the English fleet.' He flashed Admiral Canaris a significant look, as if he and Father Christmas possessed a common secret of the greatest importance. 'Then England – which cannot live without her import of food and raw materials – *will die*!'

Four

E ven after eight months of war, Dover still seemed at peace. Admittedly the white ensign flew over Dover Castle and there were anti-aircraft guns dug in on the cliffs surrounding the port. But the same old Channel ferries still plodded slowly in and out of the harbour as if this was pre-war holiday time and day trippers were enjoying a cheap trip to Calais and Boulogne. Indeed, the weather was perfect holiday weather. A beautiful blue sky fringed the sea which was, unusually, just as blue and as still as a millpond. For Mackenzie, it brought back memories of the years when he had travelled to Germany and Austria, lugging a huge suitcase filled with books and notebooks, ready for another spell of research in dusty foreign libraries, where it took three days to get a book out of the stack and there were stern warnings everywhere to remain silent.

But the tranquil air of the supply port didn't please Dalby. As the driver of the little canvas-roofed utility van changed down prior to tackling the steep hill which led to the harbour, he said harshly, 'Just look at the bloody place, Mac. You wouldn't think there was a war on, would you? Same everywhere. Able-bodied chaps who should be in the army playing bloody cricket in the fields on the way here and people off on picnics. What a ruddy Kate Karney!'

Mac allowed himself a smile. Dalby was always like that in moments of frustration and he was frustrated now by the lack of progress in the Krueger case. After all, Dalby had a reputation to live up to as the country's best and most ruthless spy catcher. He hated being defeated with a passion and he had to let off steam somehow or other. 'Let's hope we strike lucky when we get down there.' He indicated the old castle, now the command headquarters of the Straits of Dover and the local land area.

They didn't. The head of the local area Field Security Military Police was not particularly intelligent, Mackenzie thought, but he was big, bluff and impressive in that quiet but menacing manner of a professional cop which he had obviously been before the war. He *was* very professional, too. Without asking more questions than necessary, Captain Thomas told them what he knew. According to him, Dover harbour was effectively sealed off with barbed wire fencing, patrolled by both civilian, shipping and naval police. Everyone who entered the dockyard area had to show a pass and all reinforcements being sent to France to join the British Expeditionary Force there were accompanied by military policemen till they boarded the cross-channel steamers which took them to Calais and Boulogne.

'What about the sailors who crew those ferries?' Dalby asked. 'Some of the steamers will be French run as they were before the war?'

Thomas nodded his agreement, while Mackenzie stared out of the window at the port below and wondered how he might get in or out of it without a pass.

'They too have got to have passes, Major,' Thomas answered. 'Of course, knowing the French, and some of them are rum buggers who have no idea of discipline, there are some of those crewmen who pretend they've lost their passes and try to get ashore to see the – er – local tarts without them. In reality, they've sold their passes temporarily to our blokes in France who've gone on the trot' – he meant deserted – 'and are trying to get back home to the missus, or whatever.' He sighed like a man who was sorely tried. 'Naturally, we nick both the Frogs and the deserters.'

Dalby changed his tack, seemingly satisfied that the dock area was pretty secure. 'What about undesirable elements in Dover itself? Communists, for instance. They're effectively against the war since Hitler signed a pact with Stalin in Moscow last year.'

'We've got a few bolshy types here in Dover, but nothing like the situation over in Calais. The whole bloody town seems to be red. What they can sabotage of our stuff, they do. Treacherous swine.'

'Aliens?' Dalby persisted. 'Particularly German and Austrian so-called refugees?'

'Ever since Mr Churchill ordered last week to collar the lot,' the big ex-cop allowed himself a little smile at the new premier's expression, 'they've been rounded up and sent to the camps on the Isle of Man.'

'Even Jews?' Dalby asked.

'Some, who don't satisfy us they are genuine. They have been classified too as enemy aliens. But even the few who are genuine cases and have been allowed to stay in the town are under watch and have to report regularly to the local police.'

'I see,' Dalby said thoughtfully, pondering the information, while Mackenzie continued to gaze out of the window at the port below. Now a battalion of infantry had descended from the three-tonner trucks and were being served tea by green-clad girls of the local NAAFI, making the usual comments soldiers did when in the presence of women. Though Mackenzie could guess that, in reality, most of them would be nervous at the thought of the sea-journey ahead of them and the possibility they might be attacked by German U-boats known to be operating in the Channel.

Next to him, Dalby was saying, 'Well, Captain, you seem to have got Dover sewn up nice and tight. Can you suggest any other way that a potential Hun spy here might be able to communicate with his masters back in Europe, eh?'

Tho Field Security officer took his time like a good policeman should, treating the question seriously. Finally he shook his head and said, 'No, I don't think I can. We've checked the wireless angle again. Nothing doing there, Major, I'm afraid.'

'Sir,' Mackenzie butted in urgently, 'I've just thought of something.'

The two officers turned and stared at him.

'Yes, Sergeant?' Dalby said. In the presence of others he always used Mackenzie's rank; old school as he was, he tended to be very formal. As he had once told Mackenzie, 'In these matters I've always thought of Captain Scott when he was trapped in his tent in the Artic wastes with chaps of the lower deck. He drew a line across the floor of the middle of the tent and stated that one half was the upper deck reserved for officers and the other was that belonging to the lower ranks, and he didn't want the line crossed without permission.'

At the time, Mackenzie had felt the parallel was absurd and as old-fashioned as hell. Yet he understood Dalby's attitude. Still it didn't make for an easy relationship with the chief. 'Well, gentlemen, I've been looking at that battalion down there and the girls serving them their char and wads – excuse me, their tea and sandwiches.'

'Go on,' Dalby encouraged him. He knew just how bright Mackenzie was, even though he was a bit bolshy like most young people these days. After all, he had recommended him for a commission, which the young NCO would receive, once this Krueger business was solved.

'Those girls, sir. I mean they could pass on stuff to the soldiers. Let's say they'd ask them to post a letter to their boys – sweethearts – in France. I'm sure some of those reinforcements, as green as they are, would fall—'

49

Leo Kessler

'I get it,' Dalby interrupted him urgently. Turning to Captain Thomas, he asked swiftly, 'Do those NAAFI girls have a pass to get on to the docks and if they don't, how are they checked out?'

The big Field Security officer flushed red. 'Oh bollocks,' he blurted out. 'Excuse my French, sir. No, we haven't.'

Dalby said, 'Then we might just go and have a look at them. You never know, do you?'

The major's air was casual and unhurried, for which Captain Thomas was grateful; as he confessed later to Mackenzie, 'I thought I'd dropped a real clanger. I had visions of being posted to the Orkneys for the duration – and I don't like sheep one bit.' Five minutes later they had entered the dock after being duly asked to show their ID sentries (for which again Captain Thomas, fearful of that posting to those remote islands with only the sheep for company, was again grateful), and were watching the little scene in front of them.

Red-faced with the effort, the NAAFI girls, none of them very pretty, were handing out the heavy china mugs of tea, smiling at the young soldiers' puerile jokes and sexual innuendoes. They did this daily and Mackenzie could see they no longer heard the soldiers' comments. For them, the soldiers were just another group of lost boys in khaki, bound to end up as cannon fodder once the 'Phoney War' had turned into a shooting war. Mackenzie could understand the girls. What use was it investing time, love, heartache in these silly boys masquerading as soldiers who would die young and probably virginal as well? There was no future in it.

The two officers had other interests than the love life of the sweating NAAFI girls. While Mackenzie waited, they approached the manager, a fat youngish man who should have been in uniform himself, but who had obviously beaten the call-up to become manager in a reserved occupation which would ensure he'd live, undoubtedly to become

50

the general manager of a Tesco's or Sainsbury's or other supermarket of the glorious future, still yet undreamed of.

For his part, Mackenzie played the role of a bored NCO waiting for officers and gentlemen to finish their business while he twiddled his thumbs. He strolled around the dockyard listening to the girls' accents, all Kentish, as far as he could ascertain, watching them for signs of uneasines and unwarranted friendliness to the tea-swilling soldiery. But there seemed nothing out of the ordinary about them. They were simply doing a job of work. That was all.

He was just about to give up on them, telling himself it was yet another blind alley, when he spotted the girl, or more significantly her unusual hairstyle.

One of the women at the tea urns, a dark-skinned, skinny slip of a girl, had taken off the blue cap that they all wore, for some reason or other. Perhaps the hairpins that attached the cap to her hair had slipped, but she had removed the cap and was patting her hair back into shape.

He watched her do so and for a moment he couldn't take in what was strange about her particular hairstyle. Then he had it. The skinny little NAAFI had her jet-black hair styled in what the Germans called the 'cock's crow'. This was a long wave that ran the length of her head. Its style was unique to German women; perhaps because the women didn't need a hairdresser to style the 'cock's crow' for them – why, even little girls were capable of fixing their hair in this fashion, once they had given up wearing the typical little German girl's plaits.

He stared at the skinny, dark-skinned girl, his mind suddenly racing electrically, wondering how she had come to be here working for the NAAFI. For with that strange hairstyle, she could be nothing but German, though she didn't look particularly German. For a moment he was at a loss to know what to do. Could he go over and arrest a NAAFI girl just because she had a strange un-English hairstyle? The young reinforcements would probably start throwing their mugs at him.

But the way he looked at her must have alerted the skinny girl. Hastily she replaced her cap, her dark face abruptly looking very worried. She said something to the fat sweating woman next to her at the row of tea urns, the latter nodded and continued pouring mug after mug of tea. The girl wiped her hands on the dirty tea towel hanging at her waist and, before Mackenzie could react, she walked swiftly to the Ladies on the other side of the quay.

That broke the spell. Not letting his gaze deviate for a moment, he hurried over to where Dalby stood talking to Captain Thomas, as the girl disappeared into the toilet. 'Excuse me, gentlemen,' Mackenzie butted into their conversation, not standing on military ceremony.

Dalby turned and faced him immediately. 'Yes, what is it, Sergeant?'

'This, sir—'

The metallic blare of the tannoy drowned his urgent words, as the announcement began to echo from one side of the dock to the other, sending the gulls flying high in hoarse protest at being disturbed so rudely: 'The harbour authority has just been informed,' the harsh unreal voice commenced, 'that this morning the German army has attacked neutral Belgium, Luxembourg and Holland. 132 German divisions are marching south-west towards France.' There was a pause while the reinforcements froze, cups raised to their lips, caught in the act of lighting a cigarette, spitting on the cobbles. 'Now hear this. All troops will embark immediately. Off duty crews will report to their ships at once, too. RTO staff will contact the chief RTO *now*! End of message.'

Dalby broke the loud echoing silence which followed

the announcement with: 'Well, that's it. The phoney war's over . . . Now the real war has commenced.'

It was Friday, 10th May, 1940. The deadly ladies of Dunkirk could now start operating . . .

PART TWO:
THE OLD SWEAT SEES IT THROUGH

One

Next to the Old Sweat's motley collection of infantry, the artillery men were preparing to fire their last bombardment before they, too, did a bunk. He couldn't blame them. Everyone was on the run now, though General Montgomery was keeping his Iron Division, the Third, under control. Still, the Old Sweat thought the artillery were making a bit of a dog's dinner of it, as if they were back on some ruddy peacetime range in Britain. One by one the number ones were reporting their 25-pounder guns ready with: 'Number three gun ready, sir . . . Number two gun ready, sir.' It was pathetic, he told himself.

But his own command wasn't much better. Ever since the German attack had released him from the grasp of the regimental police, after that bloody business of the missing truck and the Signals corporal – poor sod – he'd been on the run. Now attired in an officer's tunic, complete with three pips and the ribbon of the Military Cross, he had somehow collected half a hundred infantrymen from the Third. There were guardsmen, East Yorks, bloody Micks from the Ulster Rifles – 'my bloody foreign legion', as the Old Sweat had called them contemptuously to himself. At first he'd tried to shoo them away. Then he realized that they were the protection from the redcaps that he needed. If the rozzers picked him, dressed as he was without papers, they'd probably top him on the spot. With a half company under his command, things would look different. He'd be an officer straggler who'd collected a bunch of other stragglers together and turned them into a fighting force. It was a good cover for getting himself back to Blighty and some little snug harbour in London with his feet under the table with a good woman. She could be bad for all he was concerned, as long as she could afford him bed and board – and more of the 'bed' than 'board'.

That was how he had become associated with this cut-off battery of Royal Artillery. As he had said to their commander, a weak-chinned subaltern who spoke very pound-notish indeed, eyeing the quods which towed their cannon, 'I'd suggest this to you. I'll give you the protection of my infantry chaps and they'll ride on your tractors or whatever you call them.'

The young officer had jumped at the chance. He'd said immediately, 'Naturally you'll have overall command.'

'Of course,' he had replied. 'Goes without saying, what.'

Now the Old Sweat wondered about his decision. The artillery officer might well be a chinless wonder with an affected voice. All the same he was obviously determined to stand and make a fight of it and it looked as though he, the veteran, who knew all the bloody angles and then some, would be forced to stand and fight with the gunners. For he couldn't just abandon them. He doubted if his infantry would stand for it. Now that they had found a leader, they were no longer stragglers, just out for number one no longer. They were British soldiers, the best in the world, or at least they thought they were.

Bollocks, the Old Sweat cursed to himself, what a frigging carry on.

It was then that the young corporal of the Grenadiers, who with two other guardsmen had taken upon himself to work a standing patrol some five hundred yards of their present position, came in, blood streaming from a wound in his shoulder. All the same, he stuck to the formula used for addressing an officer, drummed into him back at the depot: 'Permission to speak, sir?'

The Old Sweat was tempted to say something decidedly cutting, but thought better of it. The kid was hit, he was keen and more than likely he was going to get himself killed before this little lot was over. He was the type. 'Yes, get on with it. Where's the fire?'

'Over there in that copse at three o'clock. There's Jerry infantry massing there. About half a battalion, sir, I'd say.'

'Holy Mike! That's a turn-up for the books,' the Old Sweat exclaimed. Then he remembered he was an officer and gent. He changed his accent and said in his best pukka sahib manner, 'Good work, Corporal. Get a shell dressing on that wound. Tell one of your chaps to double over to the gunners and tell them what you've just reported.'

'Thank you, sir. Will do, sir,' the Grenadier replied, looking very pleased with himself, although he had suddenly become deathly pale and the blood was spurting from his shoulder in a bright sparkling red arc.

Crap, said the Lord and a thousand arseholes bent and took the strain, the Old Sweat moaned to himself in disgust. For in them days, the word of the Lord was the law. Then he forget the keen young corporal and using his glasses concentrated on the wooded area to his right.

The Old Sweat had been on the trot for three days now. He had picked up his stragglers just after Montgomery's Third Division had begun retreating from Louvain. Since then, he and his 'command' had been on the run with the Germans on their heels all the time. They had come through Ghent, crossed the French frontier near the Lys canal. For a while they thought they might stay at Petegem, which was totally empty. Cigarettes had burnt holes on the cafe tables, glasses of beer were half drained and someone had abandoned a half-finished game of draughts. The Old Sweat thought the pickings might well be gone in the dismal Flemish village, but as always the Germans had caught up with them too soon. They attacked at once as the Old Sweat realized by now they did inevitably; and just as inevitably they carried the assault. For the Old Sweat had already come to realize they were much better soldiers than the British squaddie. They mortared and sniped and 'felt' the British line for weak spots. Once they found it, they were in there with all their strength and with artillery support.

Now, as he surveyed the wood, catching fleeting glimpses of individual Germans, he realized they'd do it again here. Once the gunners had fired the last of their shells, they'd be charging across the fields, drunk or drugged or both, coming on with reckless bravery, confident that the Tommies would turn and run in the end – which they would.

The Old Sweat knew *he* had to do something in order to reverse that process. If the quads, the gun-towing tractors, were going to survive and take him and his command to safety, wherever that may be, those gunners to his left would have to save some of the last of their shells to break the German assault. Once that was done, he'd have to dissuade the chinless wonder from attempting to save his guns; now men's lives (and his in particular) were more important than four useless cannon without shells. But how?

Suddenly, startlingly, without the slightest warning, a shell burst in the air a hundred feet or so in front of the dug-in infantry. As a bright white cloud emerged in the brilliant blue morning sky, a German machine gun opened up, followed by sporadic rifle fire from the wood. The Germans were beginning their probing. Hastily the Old Sweat yelled, hands cupped about his unshaven chin, 'Hold yer frigging fire . . . The Jerries are trying it on!' He flashed a glance to where the chinless wonder was standing bolt upright ready to open fire with his 25-pounders. 'Christ,' he cursed, 'he's just tempting a ruddy Jerry sniper to pop him, silly bugger.'

'What did you say, sir?' the subaltern queried.

'Hold your fire! They're trying to draw you – and for God's sake, get down. You're standing there like a bloody spare penis at a wedding.'

A little reluctantly, or so it seemed, the officer crouched behind the armoured shield of number one gun. Just in time. Now the first mortar came shrieking out of the sky to slam into the ground ten yards away. Shrapnel rapped the gunshields like heavy tropical rain on a tin roof.

The Old Sweat turned to his own command. 'Steady lads!' he cried in his officer and gentleman's voice. 'We'll have them in due course. They'll get a packet for this, never fear.'

Now, for the next ten minutes the German mortar bombs fell steadily all around. Shrapnel hissed lethally through the air, snapping off the branches of the trees like matchwood. To their front great steaming brown holes appeared like the work of giant moles. A gun was hit. It collapsed to one side, the tyre suddenly deflated, the barrel split down the centre like a banana skin. Next to it lay the crew, dead before they had hit the ground again. The obscene stonk and blast of the mortar barrage seemed to go on for ever. Yet no one fired back. They simply crouched there trembling in their holes and pits and took it, being showered time and time again with earth, the pebbles rattling off their helmeted heads.

Then as abruptly as it had commenced, the barrage ceased. Cautiously the Old Sweat raised his head above the rim of the hole in which he huddled. Slowly the yellow smoke of the explosives was beginning to drift away. He blinked a couple of times. His vision cleared. Now he could see the first of the German infantry crouching at the edge of the wood, waiting for their orders. The Old Sweat made a quick estimate. There were at least a hundred of them. This was not going to be a skirmish line; this was going to be a company-strength attack, followed by a reserve company on one of the two flanks. He gave an unholy

61

grin. They had caught the Jerries by the short and curlies. They didn't know exactly where the British positions were, so they were going to chance it in their haste to advance, probably assuming the Tommies would do a bunk, as they had done so often before, once things got too hot for them. The Old Sweat's grin broadened. 'Not tonight, Josephine,' he whispered to himself. 'Not to-bloody-night.' He turned to the guards corporal next to him and whispered, 'Pass it on, Corp. Stand by to open fire when I give the command.'

'Sir.'

Carefully the men started to raise their heads from their holes as the order went down the line. The Old Sweat could hear them pulling back the bolts of their rifles and clicking off their safety catches. He picked up a pebble and chucked it in the direction of the chinless wonder. The latter raised his head. In dumb show, the Old Sweat pointed to his front where the Germans were now coming out of the trees. They came forward through the high grass in a slow thoughtful line like countrymen plodding to their work, deep in thought. Behind them another line of field grey appeared.

The Old Sweat nodded his head in approval. For a while he forgot his main task at this moment was to ensure that he looked after Number One: that *he* survived. Suddenly he was seized by the desire to kill, to make the Germans pay for what they had done to the British Army over the last few days. 'Jammy buggers, you think you are,' he whispered to no one in particular. 'Now yer can have another frigging think, mates.'

Now the Germans were increasing their pace. In their front and to both flanks, there were their officers and senior NCOs. Their men wore helmets, both the higher ranks wore their shiny peaked caps tilted at a rakish angle, as if they disdained death. Peering at them, the Old Sweat could see the silver skull-and-crossbones of the SS glistening in the morning sunshine, as the arrogant young bastards waved their machine pistols to encourage their men to move faster. It was as if they couldn't wait to engage the English enemy and send them fleeing in panic as they had done before.

'Look to your front,' the old Sweat hissed. The men needed no urging. The SS troopers were almost upon them now. Out of the corner of their eyes, they could see another company emerging from the trees to the left. Those would be the SS who would attempt to outflank them while the lead company pinned the defenders down. The Old Sweat had other ideas.

With another stone he alerted the chinless wonder to his intentions. He pointed to the flank attack forming and held up five fingers for five minutes. The artillery subaltern nodded his understanding. He rose to his knees and waved at his waiting gunners. The Old Sweat left him to it. He'd cope.

'All right,' he called in his normal voice. 'Five rounds rapid! Aim!'

The men brought up their rifles and did so. They could see the big solid-looking SS men quite clearly. There seemed something casual about their forward movement. It was as if they had relaxed; didn't expect any trouble. The Old Sweat's eye narrowed as he peered down the length of the rifle barrel and the blond cocky SS officer dissected by his sight. '*FIRE*!' he yelled at the top of his voice, carried away by the crazy bloodlust. He jerked the trigger. Crack! A whiff of burnt cordite. The brass butt of the Lee Enfield slammed into his shoulder. To his front the SS officer's legs started to give beneath him like those of a new-born foal. Then the still air was rent by the angry snap-and-crack of small arms fire. There were Germans, screaming, shrieking, cursing, going down to vanish into the long grass everywhere. In their positions the Old Sweat's command fired and fired, reloading magazines with hands that trembled like leaves in a high wind, shouting obscenities, yelling with triumph every time they hit a German, the bodies piling up in front of them like heaps of logs.

To their left, the chinless wonder gave that single order. Now, even he knew this wasn't a practice shoot on Salisbury plain. This was the real thing. *'FIRE!'*

The cannon roared. The gunners fired over open sights at a target they couldn't miss. The flank company of the SS hadn't a chance. It wasn't battle; it was a massacre. The Germans were slaughtered where they stood. They fell in great piles. It was sickening to look at them. Heaps of torn, limbless decapitated bodies from which came occasional groans from those who were still not dead.

But the gunners and their comrades of the infantry had no time to waste on the slaughtered Germans. They knew their time would come soon, if they didn't get out of here soon. Already the green and red distress flares were arcing into the blue sky over what was left of the Germans. They were summoning up assistance. It wouldn't be long before it appeared in the form of tanks and, even more dreaded, those Stukas of theirs which fell out of the sky like metallic hawks of hell.

Frantically the gunners fired off their last rounds, trying to set off a fire in the forest, almost as if they wanted to hide their shameful deed. The infantry, for their part, were picking up ammunition and grenades from the German corpses nearest them and doing a little looting at the same time.

The gunners had other jobs to do. As always, they had to make that terrible decision that all gunners hated: should they abandon their guns? The Old Sweat made it for them. 'You've no more shells and just taking useless guns is stupid,' he declared in his officer's voice. 'Besides, they'll use up more petrol and we're short as it is. Wherever we're going after this we'll need every drop. Right, get cracking.'

They knew what to do – there seemed to be a secret ritual

that all gunners absorbed from some source or other – but they did it reluctantly. They drew the firing pins from the breech blocks, smashed the pins on the edge of the cannon and then flung the ruined firing pins as far from the battery as possible. To make doubly sure, they dropped grenades into the upturned barrels of the 25-pounders and ran for it. The barrels split absurdly in metal leaves pointing in half a dozen different directions.

It was all over. Silently the gunners filed to the waiting quods, the drivers already gunning their engines impatiently, while the infantry, chewing on the hard German ration bread and biting off chunks of looted salami, jostled them for a place in the vehicle. For already the horizon was full of tiny black dots hurrying towards the scene of the battle. The Stukas were on their way.

Two

The whole countryside was aflutter with white. Every house, every church steeple, farm, humble cottage, even tumbledown barns had something white – a flag, a sheet, a tablecloth, even grandpa's long johns – flapping on them. The French were in a great hurry to tell the advancing Germans that they wanted to surrender. Most of the houses were heavily shuttered as they rolled past them, though the silent British had the impression that behind those bolted doors and windows anxious civilians waited for the first signs of the Boche steamroller. Then they would rush out to welcome them – as what? Conquerors or liberators? The British didn't care. They wanted to be off before 'Old Jerry' arrived.

Not that the British could escape so easily. If the civilians had gone to the ground, the rabble of the defeated French Army were still retreating; they wanted no truck with the Boche. They wouldn't fight him, but they didn't want to end up in one of his Stalags. They blocked the roads with their horse-drawn transport and the tumbledown carts, ancient Panhards, even children's prams that they had looted, often at gunpoint from the civilians, who hated them as much as they did the 'rostbifs'. Now it seemed the only soldiers they didn't hate were the Germans, who soon would make their appearance. But then they had everything to fear from the 'Fritzes'. They had been this way twice before and they remembered from the tales of their fathers and

66

grandfathers just how little nonsense the Prussians would tolerate.

The Old Sweat remembered tales, too. They were those told by his father, another canny old sweat like himself, who had been in the retreat from Mons, and four years later in March 1918 the long retreat to the coast of the defeated British Fifth Army. 'Never get caught with yer knickers down, young shaver,' the old man had lectured him over his evening jug of stout brought from the local off-licence with the money the old woman earned charring, some said whoring. 'Always be on the lookout for trouble in the making.' Well, the Old Sweat told himself now this May of 1940, they had landed up the creek without a paddle already and that was trouble enough. Yet he knew he'd have to be on the lookout for potential danger if he were going to save his own hide and, when he would admit it to himself, the men of his command.

He dodged bridges and major crossroads, for they were always bottlenecks and potential danger spots, not only as targets for the marauding Luftwaffe, which seemed to be everywhere, but also on account of the fact that there might be military police control points there with suspicious redcaps asking awkward questions. For the most part, he attempted to keep to the French D roads, with the chinless wonder doing the map reading. But it was difficult.

For it seemed the whole of the BEF was pulling back and was also trying to find the quickest and easiest way through the mass confusion. Sometimes the whole of the flat Flanders landscape was one thick mass of slow-moving transport, great long lines of trucks, tanks, Bren gun carriers, ration lorries, water bowsers stretching right to the horizon: a modern army, defeated and in retreat.

But it wasn't always on the move. Every now and again they came across convoys which had run out of petrol and from their slow-moving quods they watched as doleful soldiers smashed their trucks, knocking in the radiators with sledgehammers, slashing the tyres and then sawing them up when they were deflated. Vehicles that were near the canals that were everywhere in that part of a waterlogged Flanders were pushed into them; the canals were full of them.

Then there were the infantry, whole divisions of them, deprived of their motor transport now, slogging down the blinding-white straight roads, uniforms grey with the dust, like their fathers had done back in 1914. The soldiers were red-eyed and weary, but being British they still had to attempt the old jokes, crying, 'Some buggers have all the luck' as the quods forced their way by their files: 'Poor little gunners – they've got tender feet.' And the Old Sweat's own infantry knowing that they were on a 'cushy number', as they phrased it, kept silent and didn't look at their fellow foot-sloggers, as if they were ashamed to do so.

But the Old Sweat had other things on his mind than the hardships incurred by the 'poor bloody infantry', the PBI. He was concerned now by their destination, for it was clear that the retreating BEF was going somewhere. But where? Now and again he picked up snatches of puzzling remarks from the marching PBI: 'They say they're gunning the poor sods while they're standing neck deep in water . . . hundreds of 'em, dead and dying in the sand . . . Cor ferk a duck, it ain't fair. They ain't got a chance . . .'

The Old Sweat, normally so quick off the mark, was puzzled by what these references, caught in passing with no time to pause and ask for explanations, to some possible disaster, could be. Where were they standing 'neck deep in water' and where were they 'dying in the sand'? There was admittedly plenty of water around in the low-lying drab Flanders countryside, but there was definitely no sand. Besides, all the troops they had encountered of the beaten BEF had been moving . . . moving . . . moving . . . all the time. But to where?

That same night they reached another abandoned hamlet. There had been British troops there. They could see the green packets of five Woodbines they had left behind them in the gutters and the empty tins of M&V stew that had been tossed into the cobbled streets. But whoever the British had been, they had already departed, following the rest in lemur-like stupidity to wherever their destination might be.

But the Old Sweat made the decision that they would stay the night. It had already been bombed by the Luftwaffe and he reasoned the German planes wouldn't bomb it twice; they had targets enough to bomb for the first time. The quods were running out of petrol and as there were still civilians in the place, he reasoned they might have fuel hidden away somewhere. Besides, despite his feeling of uncertainty and growing apprehension, he felt the need 'to get his leg over', as he might have phrased it.

The chinless wonder didn't object. It was obvious that he was glad to hand over responsibility to this senior officer who wore the ribbon of the Military Cross, though he was wondering what would happen to him for having lost his guns. The Old Sweat reassured him with a crisp: 'If there were going to be court martials for what has happened here in the last few days, Lieutenant, they might well start with Gort.' He meant Lord Gort, the commander-in-chief of the BEF. 'All right, post sentries. See the men are fed and see if you can see those guardsmen out on patrol. We need to know. Me, I'm off on a shufti –' he caught himself in time, remembering he was an officer and gentlemen '– on a personal recce.'

The subaltern was only too pleased to have something to do. The Old Sweat left him handing out orders, as if he were commanding a whole brigade instead of a hundred or so beaten stragglers.

It was getting dark now. On the horizon to the west, the sky, however, flickered a pale pink. Something was going

69

on over there, the Old Sweat told himself, as for some reason he couldn't explain he drew his revolver, but what it was, he couldn't say. He could hear the muted, persistent throb of many vehicles, too. Again, all he could tell himself about them was that they were those of the defeated BEF heading west, picking up speed now as the pressure from the Luftwaffe eased.

Slowly he made his way down the Rue de Rosendaal, like the old soldier he was, sticking to the shadows cast by the peasant cottages, the only sound the crunching of broken glass under his boots as if he were walking over ice crystals on a winter's day. But there were civilians in the place, he knew that for certain now. Mysterious shadows flitted in and out between the tumbledown or ruined houses, disappearing silently around corners. He guessed they'd probably be spending the night in the cellars, once they'd looted enough grub and wine for supper. All the same, he didn't trust them. Most of them were probably communists who hated the English with a passion and would probably stab you in the back for a tanner. Maybe a few spies working for the Jerries. After his experiences in Madame Giselle's establishment in what seemed another age now, he could expect anything from the Froggies. All the same, he felt that old urge in his loins and subconsciously he rubbed his flies in anticipation, despite the danger he might be placing himself in. 'Get that heavy water off'n yer chest, old son,' he urged himself onwards, 'and yer brain'll be able to think more clear.' He pressed on.

It was about five minutes later when he was exploring the little smelly lane that ran parallel to the Rue de Rosendaal that he was stopped by the strange sound. It was a persistent rusty squeaking sort of noise, punctuated by what he took to be gasps for breath. He clicked off the .38's safety catch and stood there, head cocked to the wind in order to hear better. Slowly a grin began to form on his wizened, nut-brown old sweat's face. He knew what that sound was. Someone was dancing the mattress polka. 'Cor stone the crows,' he whispered to himself in delightful anticipation, 'I've frigging well found it!'

He frigging well had.

He crept closer to the cellar from which came that delightful noise which indicated the nearness of the source of all pleasure, and peered through the tiny dirty window hung with cobwebs. By the light of a wildly flickering candle, he made out what looked like an old man, his blue overalls down about his spindly shanks, gasping like an ancient asthmatic in the throes of a final attack, pumping the plump bottom of what appeared to be a blonde in red high-heel shoes, kneeling across the table and occasionally waggling her buttocks, as if willing the old peasant to get on with the job and be finished with it. 'Luvverly grub,' the Old Sweat whispered to himself and licked his abruptly dry lips in admiration. The old boy was certainly giving it to her – at his age.

Suddenly the peasant's spindly legs twitched, his buttocks trembled. He gave a great gasp, as if someone had just thrust a knife into his lean guts, and with one last tremor he slid off the woman's plump white buttocks and dropped to the floor, trousers still about his ankles.

The Old Sweat was inclined to applaud at first. The peasant looked every bit of eighty, yet he'd pleasured the woman as if he were a young stallion in his twenties. Then the whore, for that was what she was, raised herself and wiped the great ugly thatch of black hair at her loins before raising her head.

The Old Sweat could not repress his gasp. It was the redhead from the knocking shop, the one in Dunkirk. For a moment he could do nothing but watch as the old gaffer pulled on his blue overalls and handed the bored looking redhead a wad of greasy franc notes and then, as a kind of afterthought, picked up the basket of eggs on the floor beside him and gave her those, too.

She nodded her thanks and then with her knickers still around her ankles, she lit up a cigarette and relaxed, letting a stream of blue smoke emerge from her nostrils, while he put on his cap, touched its peak in a kind of salutation and hobbled out with the aid of a stick. She didn't seem to notice his passing, save to say, *'Ferme la porte. Il fait froid!'*

The Old Sweat was anything else but cold. He burned both with rage and desire, as he considered how he might take his revenge for what had happened to him in the Dunkirk knocking shop.

He guessed the whore wouldn't recognize him; whores never did their casual customers. All that the ladies of the night ever saw was cash and cocks in that order. Without wasting any more time, he made up his mind to tackle her. First a fuck, then the grim facts.

He opened the door of the cellar with a hearty: *'Bon soir, M'selle . . . Vous couchez avec moi maintenant?'*

It wasn't exactly a novel approach. The phrase had probably been passed down by generations of randy English soldiers ever since the time of the Napoleonic Wars. But it worked. Hastily she hoisted up her black knickers and answered in English with professional ease, 'You want jig-jig, big boy?' She smiled, revealing her gold teeth.

'You can say that agen, sweetheart,' the Old Sweat answered heartily. To himself, he said grimly, I'll give yer frigging 'big boy' later. 'How much?'

'What you want?'

'No specials,' he replied, already undoing his flies eagerly. 'Straight jig-jig . . . no frills.' He winked. 'In and out, *compris*?'

She leered at him. *'Compris.'* But her cunning, calculating eyes didn't light up.

Routinely she slipped her black knickers down once more.

She brushed up her great bush of black hair and settled over the table once more, legs spread wide again. 'You ready?' she asked.

Gleefully, the plan forming at the back of his mind forgotten for the moment, the Old Sweat pulled out his already rampant penis like a policeman's truncheon and chortled, 'Am I ready? You betcha yer life I am, missus.'

She gave a grunt, as if she were already enjoying him penetrating her. He ignored it. It was just part of the act; he knew that.

He grunted himself now, but with real pleasure as he thrust his penis into her. 'Hold tight, you bitch,' he hissed through gritted teeth. 'This is it!' He surrendered himself to the pleasures of the flesh, all else forgotten, while over on the horizon which was Dunkirk and the sea, the flames flickered higher and higher and what was left of the British Expeditionary Force prepared to meet its doom.

Three

'Remember gentlemen,' the silver-haired admiral said severely, 'what I am about to tell you is most secret. If any officer present here reveals anything of what I shall say, I shall personally see he is court-martialled, cashiered and sent to prison. Is that quite clear?'

The assembled officers from the Navy, RAF and Army, who were crowded in Admiral Ramsey's office in the castle carved out of the chalk cliffs five hundred feet above Dover, mumbled their agreement and waited, wondering why they had been summoned here so urgently this May morning and with so much secrecy.

Major Dalby, standing at the back of the tight room, could guess what it was: over the last forty-eight hours while they had searched for the missing NAAFI girl (the only lead they had so far), Dalby had heard some disquieting rumours from the other side of the Channel. Still, he waited patiently for what Ramsey, Flag Officer Commanding Dover, had to say.

The big bluff admiral wasted no time. He said, 'Gentlemen, I can inform you that at this moment some 400,000 British and French soldiers are in full retreat out of Belgium, where our ally, the Belgian Army, has completely collapsed – we expect the King of Belgium to surrender at any moment.'

Even the regulars, hardened as they were and trained to expect bad news in battle, gasped.

Ramsey didn't comment. He continued immediately: 'At the present time, the BEF and the French troops with them, possess a German-free corridor some fifty miles long and about fifteen miles wide leading to the old port of Dunkirk – Calais is already surrounded by the Boche. On the face of it, as things stand at the moment and if we don't do anything, approximately 300,000 British troops will be German prisoners of war by the weekend.'

Again his audience couldn't restrain their shock. The officers gave another gasp. Even Dalby, who had been through so much during his four years in the trenches in the 'old war' could not fight off his sense of shock. A whole British army, the only one capable of fighting the Hun, wiped out within a week. It was hardly possible. But the look on the Admiral's face told him it was.

'We face, in essence, a nightmare scenario,' Ramsey continued. 'Either we do something, or if we don't we just sit on our damned thumbs and watch our army on the Continent tamely go into the bag. The men we might possibly be able to replace, but their equipment . . .' Ramsey shrugged his shoulders, as if he simply could not go on with his recital of woe. 'But,' he raised his voice, as if to indicate there was still a chance, 'we don't intend to sit on our thumbs and simply let it happen. Our new prime minister Mr Churchill is a real fighting cock. He has ordered me to bring off as many of our men as possible. It will mean the end of the war in France and it will be a great defeat for the British Army – make no mistake of it – but if we pull it off, we will still have an army.' He paused, his big chest heaving with the effort of so much talk.

Down below there was a ship siren's howling like some lost sea creature in dire pain. The mournful sound penetrated into the packed room and Dalby thought it seemed to signify something: the beginning of a tragedy, which wouldn't be limited to the British Army in France, but which would go on, perhaps for the rest of his life. He was unable to define the feeling accurately. All the same, he knew that something terrible was going to happen.

'Now,' Ramsey went on, 'the only French harbour of strategic importance in our hands is that of Dunkirk. Dunkirk is already undergoing round the clock bombing, as if the Boche know our intentions. However, it is surrounded by twenty-five miles of bloody awful coastline. It used to be called the "graveyard of ships" and it's unapproachable with large craft. That, gentlemen, is where we're going to attempt to bring off the British Army.' His hard gaze circled their faces, as if trying to etch each and every one of them on his mind's eye. 'It's going to be bloody hard and we can only use small ships to get the soldiers off, but we're going to have a damn good crack at it, what!'

'Here, here!' There was a burst of enthusiasm from the assembled officers at Ramsey's brave, bold words and although Dalby felt the army really didn't stand a cat's chance in hell once the Boche let their air force loose on the trapped squaddies, he, too, was stirred by Ramsey's determination. He told himself that if anyone could pull it off, it had to be the big Admiral.

'For the moment then, that is the situation,' Ramsey started to end the top secret meeting. 'We'll take them off the best we can at makeshift piers and the like. To do the job we have forty destroyers and about 150 armed merchantmen. It's not enough, when you think the warships are packed with guns and the like so there's not much damned space for troops. We'll have to find more craft somewhere, even if they are civilian. But we'll worry about that later. For the time being, I can tell you this. The mission, we're calling it "Operation Dynamo", commences at first light tomorrow morning.' He took off his glasses and slapped shut his book of notes. 'That's all, gentlemen. Let's get on with it.'

'Attention!' someone cried.

The officers clicked to attention.

Admiral Ramsey, who wouldn't survive the war, put on his gold-edged cap and touched his hand to its brim. Then he swept out followed by his staff officers.

Mackenzie was waiting for Dalby as the officers, excitedly chatting among themselves, left the room. Dalby waited for them to clear. Then he took the staff sergeant by the elbow and steered him into the far corridor, away from the clerks and the ATS typists busy in their offices, presumably preparing for Operation Dynamo.

'Listen, Mac, something big is about to happen. We're going to have to drop the present business for a while. We'll need to have top level security here in Dover now—'

'Sir,' Mackenzie interrupted him hastily, 'can I say this first?'

Dalby nodded. 'Fire away then, but make it snappy. We have a lot to do this day.'

'It's this, sir. Whoever she is, she's disappeared – and the NAAFI have no records of her.'

'You mean the girl with the German hairdo, Mac?'

'Yessir. But there's more, sir. Field Security – Captain Thomas – called me while you were in conference.' Mackenzie frowned for some reason or other. Perhaps he didn't like reminding himself of what he had just learned.

'Get on with it, Mac,' Dalby urged impatiently.

'The Radio Location people told him that there is an illegal transmitter operating in the general Dover area. They reckon it's beamed on the area of Hamburg and you know what that means, sir?'

'Yes, I do,' Dalby answered grimly. 'At Wohltorf just outside Hamburg, the *Abwehr* have their major radio station. The illegal transmitter is Jerry all right. Do they have a fix on the pianist?'

'No, sir. Looks like he's a first-class concert pianist. Hardly on the air for more than a minute, so Captain

Thomas says. By the time the Radio Location people had picked him up and were trying to get a fix on him, he was off the air and up and running.'

Dalby was silent for a moment, while Mackenzie noted how old his chief was getting. This new war was beginning to place a severe strain on him. He was one of the few desk-bound officers that Mackenzie knew who took his job very seriously. During the phoney war period most of the non-regulars had thought it was all a bit of a joke: a chance to get away from the old woman and enjoy themselves in the mess or with another younger model. Not Dalby; he fought his part of the war as if every hour counted if they were going to beat the Hun.

Finally Dalby spoke. 'This throws things into a new light, Mac,' He lowered his voice so that Mackenzie had to strain to hear him. 'Keep this under your hat. They'll have me court-martialled if they find out at this moment that I've told you. They're going to evacuate the BEF through Dunkirk.'

Mackenzie looked aghast. 'You mean, we're doing a bunk, sir?'

'Exactly.' There was no mistaking the bitterness in his voice. 'The Hun has beaten us in the very first round.' He shook his head. 'God knows where it's all bloody well going to end.' With an effort, Dalby pulled himself together. 'Mac, what you have just told me puts a different complexion on the matter in hand.'

'How do you mean, sir?'

'This. Overnight, it seems, Dover has become a very important place, militarily speaking. The evacuation via Dunkirk is going to be directed by Admiral Ramsey, who is, as you know, based here. It might be just a coincidence, but I don't think it is. Now, it seems, the Hun has seemingly got a new pianist in the place of Krueger and he's working from Dover – just at the very same time that the port becomes so very important.' He emphasized the words harshly. 'Now, Mac, what does that tell you?'

Mackenzie was quick off the mark. 'Well, you don't need a crystal ball to deduce that the two events are connected.'

'Exactly.

'Someone starts sending info to *Abwehr* headquarters in Hamburg, from where, as we know, they direct espionage operations against the UK, just when this place becomes vital to our attempt to save the British Army in France. It certainly can't be a coincidence. We might assume further, sir, that the German agent is concentrating on our shipping from—' He stopped suddenly.

'Go on,' Dalby urged him, 'what were you going to say?'

'I don't know exactly, sir, but we might be dealing with shipping from both Dover and Dunkirk. And if we are, what is the German link between the two places, eh?'

But at that moment there seemed no answer to that overwhelming question . . .

Four

They had been forced to abandon the first of the quods some ten miles from Dunkirk. They had run out of petrol. The remaining vehicles had been forced off the road a few miles further on by the protests of the stalled weary infantry who packed the road. The footsloggers had shouted angrily at them, 'Pull in . . . pull in, yer cheeky sods . . . Wait your turn like the rest of us.' It was if they were jealous of their place in what seemed a gigantic queue. For what, the Old Sweat didn't know.

What he did know, however, was that he didn't want a scene with the infantry just now. It might attract the attention of the redcaps who seemed to be everywhere, trying to keep some sort of order as more and more streamed in to come to a weary stop behind those already waiting there. It was bad enough having the redheaded whore 'under close arrest', escorted everywhere, even when she squatted brazenly in the ditches to urinate, by the embarrassed Grenadier corporal and two of his guardsmen. Even the weariest of the squaddies standing in line took notice of her when she appeared. No, he told himself as he gave orders to drive the quods into the ditch and have their radiators smashed and drained, better walk and keep a low profile, old mate. That's the only way yer gonna survive this particular balls-up.

But progress was slow. The infantry moved in single file on both sides of the country road at a snail's pace, while the centre was packed with demoralized civilians carrying their pathetic bits and pieces mixed with dirty, unshaven poilus, many of whom had already thrown away their rifles. Red-eyed and dust-begrimed, the soldiers marched a few paces and then came a sudden halt, which often lasted ten or fifteen minutes before they could go on again only to repeat the process. It was during these enforced breaks that the Old Sweat, playing his role as an officer trying to cheer up the common soldiers, picked up scraps of conversations which gave him some idea of what was going on ahead. 'Some have been on the beach for three days before they took 'em off . . . They gun the blokes even when they're swimming to the lifeboats. Hundreds of dead and dying lying on the sands . . . poor sods, didn't have a chance . . .'

As the Old Sweat put it together, the Royal Navy was beginning to take off the beaten BEF, or what was left of it, from the long beaches on both sides of the port of Dunkirk. To him it looked like it was going to be first come, first served and although he heard that some of more intact infantry battalions were forming a last ditch perimeter which would be held until everyone was taken off, he had not seen any of these suicide candidates yet – and who could tell whether they'd be able to hold out that long once the Jerries brought up their tanks, which they would do in due course.

All that long May afternoon while the dismounted gunners and his command trudged slowly forward to those fatal beaches, the Old Sweat mulled the problem over in his mind, though his wizened brown face revealed nothing of his inner turmoil. To any observer, especially if that observer was a hard-eyed suspicious redcap, he was a typical good regular officer cheering up his weary men, now and again taking a rifle from some footsore straggler and carrying it for him for a while, always leading with a word of encouragement.

Sooner or later if he continued in this present role, he knew he would end up on those deadly beaches, perhaps becoming one of those 'hundreds of dead or dying lying on the sands'. But he was not a 'poor sod without a chance'. He was the Old Sweat, who had survived this long on his wits and fully intended to survive longer. It stood to reason, therefore, that the time was soon coming when he had to get rid of the chinless wonder's gunners and his own command. Otherwise he would be saddled with them, and waiting on these beaches.

He reasoned that the redheaded whore, who kept throwing sullen angry glances in his direction, was his way out. But he had to do it in a bold, if chancy, manner which would convince a senior officer that he and his 'prisoner' should have priority in boarding one of the rescue vessels.

He sucked his upper set of false teeth thoughtfully as he mulled over the problem. It was getting dark now, the sky to the west a mottled golden scarlet as the flames from the last German bombing raid grew higher and higher. It was clear that the Luftwaffe had hit an oil dump of some kind before departing, the day's bombing over now that darkness was falling. By the light of the flames he could make out shadowy figures in fields to left and right, stolidly digging slit trenches with officers giving quiet orders (as if they didn't want to upset the rabble plodding by to the beaches), where to site mortars and machine guns. This was the perimeter. This was where they would fight the last battle before the Germans swept the suicide candidates aside and rushed the undefended beaches.

The sight quickened the Old Sweat's thought processes. He had known the redheaded whore was a 'rum 'un' back in Dunkirk, when he had woken up from his doze after 'slipping her a link' to find her gone, his tunic pockets opened, and had heard the voices outside conversing in a guttural language which he had known instinctively wasn't French.

At first he'd thought she'd been up to the usual whore's

tricks: rifling his money while he had a little shut-eye. But he had found his remaining money was still intact, yet his Army paybook and AB 64, which contained his vital military statistics, were gone. For a minute that had puzzled him. What good were they to a whore? She couldn't sell them on the black market.

But then he had remembered that when she had been playing with his penis at the very beginning and he had been wondering whether what he had in mind for her would be regarded as an extra, she had asked casually, 'You in Signals?' His mind had been too full of the certain perversion that he was about to propose to her and he had not paid much attention to the question. Now it struck him that it was very strange for a whore to ask that sort of a question, and not long after that he had concluded with a certain feeling of apprehension that this particular knocking shop might well be a base for enemy spies. Why would she or one of the other 'hoors' be outside the blackout talking what he thought was German?

Now as he trudged along with the rest of the beaten British Army, the pieces of the jigsaw seemed to fall into place rapidly: the redhead's strange behaviour; the disappearance of the young corporal after he had done a bunk; the fact that she had been in the village along the BEF's main line of retreat. Had it just been a coincidence that she had been in that ruined barn shagging the old Frog – or had she been planted there to observe the retreating British Army for some reason known to her bosses in Berlin?

The Old Sweat felt a sudden anger at the two-timing bitch. She ought to be strung up from the nearest tree, he told himself in abrupt fury. But at the same time he felt, too, that she might well be the way he could work his ticket to Blighty. Naturally he could just hand her over to Field Security and let them interrogate her. But what good would that do him? No, the Old Sweat concluded, suddenly quite happy, though his feet hurt like hell and he was getting bloody tired of playing the officer and gent; it was too strenuous. Play it right, he told himself, and he might well be in Blighty by this time tomorrow. Hold on to the redhead (who was just at that moment standing with her legs apart and her knickers around her ankles urinating like a man in a gush of golden steaming liquid, much to the admiration of the nearest soldiers who could see her in the glowing darkness), and he'd be eating steak and chips, washed down with a pint of best bitter in Whitehall before the day was out. 'Luvverly grub,' he muttered to himself as he shuffled into the night with the rest.

'A Company, East Yorks,' they were shouting. 'Over here, A Company . . . Rally on me. HQ Company, Green Howards . . . KOSBs over here . . . Look smartish, the King's Own Scottish Borderers . . .' As they straggled through the dunes, with exhausted men lying everywhere on the sand, they could see the whole front of Dunkirk still ablaze from the air raid and the mortar bombs exploding on the dying port. To the front there were gaunt wrecks of paddle steamers and freighters next to the black wall of the mole stretching from the beach far out into the sea. Next to it, there were line after line of soldiers thrown into sudden relief by the exploding bombs and sudden spurts of cherry-red flames, standing, some of them, up to their necks in the water, waiting for the boats which would transport them to the steamers and destroyers barely glimpsed further out to sea. It reminded the Old Sweat of the pre-war football crushes outside the turnstiles of the grounds. But these men were strangely patient, as if they were too exhausted to shove and push. Or perhaps they had just lost the will to live and were hoping that someone would take on that responsibility for them.

The Old Sweat had seen enough. As he halted his command, he cursed under his breath, 'Fuck this for a game of soldiers . . . I'm off.' Louder, he said to the Grenadier Guards' corporal. 'I'll take over custody of the prisoner now. I'll hand her over to the proper authorities.'

'Sir!' the guardsman snapped to attention and slapped the butt of his rifle smartly in salute, as if he were back in his red coat in front of Buckingham Palace.

The Old Sweat turned to the subaltern, who didn't look very happy. 'You take over temporary command, Lieutenant. Get the men down to the water. Maintain discipline. Use your revolver if you have to. Is that clear?'

The chinless wonder's bottom lip trembled and the Old Sweat thought he might cry, but he pulled himself together and answered bravely enough. 'Very clear, sir,' he said, then remembering the guardsman's salute, he, too, clicked to attention and did the same.

Inwardly, the Old Sweat groaned and told himself, Bullshit still reigns supreme in the old Kate Karney. Then he was off, leaving them to their fate, quickening his pace, despite his sore feet, as if he couldn't get off that doomed beach fast enough.

Fifteen minutes later he found himself in a large basement, packed both with British soldiers and a motley group of dirty unshaven French civilians and soldiers, waiting to be interrogated by a grim-faced officer in the Field Security Police. He sat at a trestle table, with a drawn revolver lying on it, while around him heavily armed redcaps, who the Old Sweat knew usually formed a firing squad on these occasions, waited like vultures to seize their victim and shoot him to death at the nearest wall.

In the recesses of the basement, there were soldiers who had broken down, making strange little animal noises, while a sergeant with the ribbons of the old war was crying openly, his hands clasped over his eyes. The Old Sweat told himself that if the redcaps had their way, they'd be shot as well.

He dismissed the shell-shock victims. He had a role to

play and it needed all his attention and experience, based on years of swinging the lead, to do it. He waited a moment while the grim-faced Field Security officer – a captain – dealt with one suspect. He looked down briefly at the man's ID card, then snapped in good French, 'You were seen to enter a house on the edge of Dunkirk wearing a uniform. You later reappeared in civvies and carrying a box. It contained a portable wireless set, according to a witness.'

The dirty little Frenchman, if that was what he was, raised his arms upwards as if appealing to God in heaven Himself. 'It's a lie, *mon General*,' he protested excitedly.

The hard-faced captain was not impressed by the '*mon General*' or the dirty-faced man's protest. 'We will see about that,' he said grimly, and then in English to the redcap sergeant, 'take him away.'

'To shoot him?' the NCO asked eagerly, his red face lighting up. It was as if he couldn't get the suspect stood against the wall in front of a firing squad soon enough.

The Field Security officer shook his head a little wearily. 'No, hand him over to the gendarmes. They can deal with him.' Then he seemed to become aware for the first time of the Old Sweat and his sullen-faced redheaded prisoner. He half-rose from his chair and asked, 'How can I help you, sir? Do you want me to take her off your hands, sir?' He indicated the whore.

The Old Sweat plunged in rapidly. 'Thank you, but no, Captain,' he said firmly. 'Please come over here.' He indicated the corner where the old sergeant was still sobbing. 'I have something for your ears only.'

The captain sighed wearily, but complied, saying to the redcap NCO, 'Get rid of old Bill there, will you please.'

A moment later the Old Sweat was telling the captain his story in a hurried whisper, while the latter listened, his red-rimmed eyes as wary and as suspicious as ever. But the Old Sweat was at his most persuasive and when he was finished with his tale, the captain asked, 'So you think, sir, that this is something bigger than the usual petty agent stuff?'

'I do,' the Old Sweat answered with supreme confidence, but inwardly praying fervently that the hard-pressed captain would accept his story and have him on board one of the rescue vessels before the former started to mull over and find fault with what he had just told him. 'Indeed I am risking being court-martialled, I must tell you, by leaving my chaps under the leadership of my second-in-command – a stout fellow though – to carry out this self-imposed task. But I feel so strongly about it. I must report directly to the War Office.'

'All right, sir.' The captain rose stiffly. 'I'll write you out a chitty.' He nodded to the redhead. 'What about her? Do you want one of my chaps as escort for her for the crossing?'

Hurriedly the Old Sweat shook his head. He tapped his revolver holster significantly. 'I'll soon put madam in her place if she starts acting up, I can assure you, Captain.'

'Very well, sir. I'll get you on your way.'

Five minutes later the Old Sweat, now with the redhead handcuffed to his left wrist, was being driven by two heavily armed redcaps, who looked as if they'd stand no nonsense from the thousands of troops packed everywhere, to the waiting cross-Channel paddle steamer, its engines already throbbing impatiently.

Behind him, Dunkirk burned in its death agonies. But the Old Sweat didn't look back; his gaze was fixed firmly to his front where Blighty lay. Jammy bugger, he said to himself in self-congratulation as he urged the woman up the gangway, 'You've gone and done it a-bloody-agen!' And he had.

Five

Admiral Ramsey looked tired and worn – there were dark circles due to lack of sleep and the awesome responsibility he had taken upon himself to save a whole British army. Still, Dalby, waiting for the Admiral to speak, could see the bluff broad sailor was fully in control, though it was pretty obvious that things were getting out of control. As he looked out of the window of Ramsey's office high above the Channel, he could see the badly damaged destroyer just outside the harbour, listing heavily to port with black smoke pouring from her damaged aft, proceeding at no more than a couple of knots.

The destroyer returning from Dunkirk was not the only damaged ship in sight. A mile or so out, one of the pre-war ferries was sinking slowly with men jumping panic-stricken into the sea all around her, while the local boats hurried from shore to save them. Dalby frowned. Such scenes had been commonplace around Dover ever since the evacuation of the BEF had commenced three days ago.

Ramsey raised his head from his papers and said, 'Have a gasper, Dalby.' He pushed the silver cigarette case across the desk towards the Intelligence major. 'Sorry to keep you waiting, but all hell has been let loose lately, I'm afraid.'

'I understand, sir,' Dalby answered, taking one of the cigarettes – naturally it was a Senior Service – and lighting it.

Ramsey took one too, but didn't light it. It was as if he

had already forgotten it. Instead, he just kept the cigarette between his fingers unlit as he continued: 'I can tell you, Dalby, our losses are very high. In these last three days, the Hun has already sunk twenty of my destroyers and perhaps twice that number of armed merchantmen.'

Dalby nodded sympathetically. He already knew that the Navy's losses off Dunkirk had been so high that the naval authorities had appealed to anyone who had a boat to report for duty to take off the stranded soldiers. The response had been tremendous. Civilians, several in their seventies, even eighties, had turned up in everything from red-sailed nineteenth-century Dutch fishing smacks to totty motorboats with names like *Lubelle* and *Zuleika* that had never been further than a couple of miles down the Thames.

'Now, the reason I've called you in, Dalby, is this,' the Admiral continued as the sirens commenced their dreary wail over Dover yet again. 'The Hun seems to be able to predict the movement of our naval vessels too accurately. I understand that the Huns can make educated guesses when we move from Dover or Dunkirk – the tides, high and low water at Dunkirk and all that. But even when we move at night when their air force normally stands down, out of the blue up comes their bloody Stukas and Junkers and starts the same old business of knocking the living daylights out of my destroyers.' He ran his big hand across his brow like a man who is being sorely tried and Dalby noticed the hand shook a lot.

As the Stukas appeared on the horizon to the east and began to form up for their usual death-defying dive-bombing attack and the ack-ack artillery commenced their first defensive barrage, Dalby asked, 'With what you have just said, I take it, sir, that you think there is a security leak here and possibly in Dunkirk too?'

'Yes, I do. I have managed to find time to read your reports to your HQ at the War Office and I saw yesterday that you report that there is an illegal transmitter operating in the general Dover area.'

Now it was Dalby's turn to be a little flustered. 'Yessir. We're going all out to try to locate it. The radio detection boys are working round the clock in three eight-hour shifts waiting for the operator to go on air and locate him. But their pianist—'

'Pianist?'

'Wireless operator, sir.'

'I see. Carry on.'

'Well, he's so nifty and expert, really high-class top-level morse, tapped out at a tremendous rate, that he transmits and goes off air before we can detect him.' Dalby shook his head. 'We'll get him sooner or later, but for the moment . . .' He left the rest of the sentence unsaid, as if he were too exasperated to try to explain any further.

'I understand, Dalby. Direction finding and location are damned hard at the best of times. I know, I've done it at sea. So I'm going to help your people. There's a DF team at Pompey waiting to be sent up to Scapa to man a new battleship there. But the ship's not ready. They're being sent here to Dover to help in the meantime. I've also asked Harwich if they can let me have a crew from the cruiser squadron stationed there. Anything I can get you, Dalby, you shall have.' There was no denying the urgency in Ramsey's words now. Obviously the situation of the destroyer fleet in the Channel was nearing disaster. 'But I beg you, Major, find these Huns ASP and put a stop to this matter.' Ramsey forced a smile. He waved a hand. 'Sorry, Dalby, that's all the time I can spare you. War to be won – all that sort of rot.'

Dalby sprang to attention, put on his cap hurriedly and saluted. But the Admiral had already forgotten him. He was bent over his papers once more, scribbling furiously.

Outside, Mackenzie was waiting for him in the Admiral's little ante-room, listening to the muted thunder of the flak outside as the first of the Stuka prepared to peel off and commence the dive-bombing attack. He shook his head as soon as Dalby emerged and the older officer knew what that meant; he still hadn't found the girl with the German hairstyle.

Dalby nodded his understanding and hastily put his NCO in the picture. Quickly the two of them prepared a new detection plan to use the new men being drafted in. The major said, 'We'll tie up Dover from the Eastern Docks down to the western ones. Circle that area with all available detection vans on the high ground between the Dover Road and the Folkestone one. That means, if the pianist is transmitting in the old town itself and tries to do a runner, we're above him and can spot anyone who looks suspicious. If he goes to ground in the old town, well, we've got him by the short and curlies.'

'Agreed, sir, and remember the Provost Marshal has thrown a cordon between West Cliffe and right over to Capel le Ferne to nab any deserter from the boats bringing them back from Dunkirk trying to head for the big smoke.'

'Yes, there are too many of the cowardly buggers,' Dalby said bitterly. 'They think we've lost the damned war already. No matter,' he dismissed the deserters. Then he added: 'One major point is now to be considered, Mac. If, as the Admiral thinks, and I tend to agree with him, that someone is signalling the departure of our warships and other vessels from both Dover and Dunkirk, how is the Dunkirk side getting the messages to the *Abwehr* in Wohltorf?'

'Agreed, sir. All the Field Security policemen will be concentrating now in the Dunkirk area and so far there have been no reports of a pianist in that area.'

'Exactly, Mac.' Dalby had regained his old keenness. His eyes shone like those of a well trained hunting dog that has picked up the scent and a possible trail. 'So we can possibly assume – as we know there *is* a pianist here in Dover – that it's from here that ship sailings from both ports are being reported back to the enemy. We wind up Dover and we cripple Dunkirk at the same time, eh, Mac.'

'Yessir. But first we've got to find the bloody Dover pianist,' Mackenzie said, suddenly miserable. 'And so far we haven't had much luck. If only we could find that girl with the hair—'

He never finished the sentence. Suddenly, and rather foolishly, a young signals corporal was running down the corridor outside, bare-headed, seemingly very excited and whirring an air-raid rattle, almost as if he were a too enthusiastic spectator at some pre-war cup final, shouting, 'Everybody outside who can swim! Passenger steamer going down with chaps from Dunkirk in the harbour . . . Everybody outside who can swim for rescue party . . . outside . . .' And then he was gone clattering down the stone-flagged corridor in his hobnailed boots.

It was only later that the younger man, Mackenzie, realized that the signals corporal was wearing the black-and-red triangular patch of the Third Infantry Division – and Montgomery's Third was still on the other side of the Channel!

The Old Sweat had started to become amorous. It was the combination of relief, a half bottle of whisky that a drunken officer had handed him as he had boarded the boat with the redhead handcuffed to him, and her very close proximity under the blanket they had draped over their shoulders in the crowded ferry. Indeed the boat was so crowded that they could hardly move an inch, but he had used his rank and the important embarkation tag given him by the Field Security captain to get the two of them ensconced on a battered leather sofa that someone had placed on the weak, slippy deck. There, animated by sudden sexual desire engendered by the fiery spirit surging through his body, he had offered her a limp Woodbine and a slug of his scotch.

She had taken them, keeping her eyes half-closed as she drunk the whisky straight from the bottle so that he couldn't see the look of hatred in them. Nor did she pull back when he covered his loins with the khaki blanket that smelled of horses and placed her hand on his genitals. She knew what to do. She undid his stiff brass fly buttons and thrust her hand inside his underpants.

The Old Sweat gave a little sigh of what sounded like relief and slumped back further. Not more than a couple of feet away the exhausted survivors of the great Dunkirk debacle seemed unaware of what was going on under the blanket. Perhaps, if they did, they didn't care. Sex was not important at this moment, just survival.

Not the Old Sweat. He'd survived. Now he wanted to enjoy the fruits of survival. 'More!' he gasped, as she started pumping his erect penis up and down. 'Come on, give it some stick.' He groaned with pleasure, eyes screwed tightly shut now, as if he didn't want any part of the miserable world all about him.

'*C'est difficile*,' she protested. 'Left hand no good. Right better.'

'Bollocks,' he cursed. 'All right.' Still keeping his eyes shut, he slipped the key into the cuffs and opened them. 'Come on now. Don't waste no more time. Chop . . . chop.'

Sale con anglais, she muttered under her breath. Aloud, she said, as she spat on the palm of her right hand. 'Yes, yes . . . I make it nice for you, Tommy.'

He relaxed again, as her damp hand sought and grasped his erection. 'Cor stone the crows!' he sighed, 'that's bleeding good!'

Her face twisted with hate, her gaze searching for a way out before it was too late. She commenced working on him once more, taking it more slowly and pleasurably for him now, prolonging the time she would be freed from the handcuffs.

All around her men snored, sighed, farted, muttered faintly, stuttered a few phrases she didn't understand: 'Hellfire, if I could only get me socks off . . . Our A Company took a bloody hard knock . . . wiped out I hear . . . Got a fag, mate . . . I need a spit-and-a-draw to soothe my nerves . . . Get yer frigging boot out of me guts, willyer . . .'

Nothing there. Then she heard it and knew she still had a chance. It was the bass moan of the ship's foghorn. She'd heard the sound often enough in the months she had worked in Dunkirk for the German woman. The old ferry was signalling she was about to enter harbour. Her heart leapt. That was the way out. Next to her, the Old Sweat had thrown his head back, his mouth open and slack with pleasure. She leaned over. She pressed the tip of her tongue in and out of his parted lips. At the same time, she increased the speed of her hand under the blanket. She could feel his heart pressed close to her side beating furiously with the passion of it all. '*Now . . . now . . . please*!' he choked as she pressed her cunning tongue ever deeper into his throat. 'Oh for God's sake, let me come . . .'

She smiled cruelly. With her left hand, she detached the jack knife that hung at his belt, with her thumb nail, she flicked open the blade. You'll not come, she told herself maliciously, you'll go!

Now it was almost over. The ship's horn had subsided. She could hear the sound of aeroplane engines just overhead. She took no notice of them; she was too intent on what she had to do in the very next instant. She took a firmer grip on the handle of the jack knife. His body heaved, his head turned crazily to one side. His face was flushed and ugly, glazed with sweat. He began to tremble as if in the grips of some raging fever. Then it happened.

Not as she had expected, however. In the same instant that he ejaculated, the bomb struck the bows of the old Channel ferry. The ship shuddered violently. In a flash she was listing to port. Men shouted. Others cursed. Up on the deck, the alarm bells began to ring urgently. An official voice yelled urgently, 'Abandon ship . . . Hear this, abandon ship!'

Thick black choking smoke began to drift through the stateroom. She pulled her hand away from him, as if his now flaccid organ was red hot. He called something which she didn't understand. She sprang to her feet. The ship lurched violently once more. She caught herself from falling just in time. A sergeant grabbed hold of her. He was drunk. His breath stank of whisky or rum. 'Let me help, luv,' he said thickly, hands reaching instinctively for her ample breasts. She pushed him to one side. He staggered and fell full length over the Old Sweat who was under the blanket still. She clawed and fought her way to the stairs. Frantic, frightened soldiers were doing the same on all sides. It was every man for himself now.

'Stop that French cow!' the Old Sweat cried, throwing back the blanket and trying to do up his flies. 'She's a spy!'

No one was listening.

Madly she pushed her way on to the crazily tilting deck. There were broken shattered men lying on all sides in pools of their own bright red blood. Above, a broken funnel erupted thick, choking, black smoke. Chaos on all sides. Through a gap in the smoke, she saw men belting down the length of the jetty. *The rescuers*, flashed through her mind. She was going to be saved, come what may. The English swine would be drowned down below. She'd become another poor Belgian refugee. The foolish English would accept her, beneath their hard exterior, they always had a soft spot. She grinned. Even as she did so, the mast

95

started to rend and tear. She looked up. The grin turned to fear. She blanched. She raised her arms in front of her upturned face. '*NON!*' she screamed and then all was darkness . . .

PART THREE:
THE JEWESS

One

O n that terrible November day in 1938 when the brown-shirted mob from Trier had arrived in the Pariserplatz and had begun drinking at Neubergers in between throwing bricks at the windows of Hermann Bachs, the biggest store in Wittlich, and howling for 'Yiddish blood', her father had taken off his white medical apron, dismissed his remaining patients and retired to his changing room.

For a while she and her terrified mother thought he might do something horrible to himself. He still had his World War One uniform in the cupboard there and his wartime revolver, too, fully loaded. They had been mistaken. *Herr Medizinalrat* Dr Jacobsohn, *Rittmeister* of the Death's Head Hussars (retd), was not going to give in that easily.

Fifteen minutes later, as the riot outside in the little Moselle township had grown ever louder and there was already the smell of burning torches as if they were preparing to burn down the Jewish centre of the place, Father had appeared dressed in his old wartime Hussar uniform. On any other occasion he might well have been regarded as a comic figure in his gold-rimmed glasses and uniform bulging at the stomach, which contrasted so strongly with the bold busby and insignia of the elite daring Death's Head Hussars. Not now. For here was a Jew venturing out into the mob, a lone elderly figure in a crowd of bloodthirsty thugs in the brown uniforms of Hitler's anti-Semitic Storm Troopers.

His appearance caught them off guard, especially the local

SA men, all of whom knew the Jewish doctor; indeed many of them had been brought into the world by Dr Jacobsohn and cured of their childish ailments by a man who never really pressed hard for payment for his services. Here and there some of them took off their peaked caps in a sign of respect or gave him a military salute. For on his breast, the doctor bore the Iron Cross First Class and other wartime orders for bravery and all of them knew that the reason the doctor wore glasses was that he had an eye shot out on the Russian front back in 1915.

Doctor Jacobsohn didn't seem to notice. Head held high, he walked through the locals who drew back to make his way free, heading straight for the synagogue, where already the ruffians from Trier, who had been specially brought in for this task, were preparing to lay fire to it, while others flung stones at the windows breaking the glass in an orgy of wanton destruction.

He got closer and closer. Here and there the leaders of the Trier SA, who had organized the mob, started to turn and stare in wonder at this lone middle-aged Jew in his ill-fitting uniform from the days of the Kaiser, who dared to venture on to the streets at a time like this. Here and there the locals whispered fearfully, 'Don't go, *Herr Doktor* . . . it's dangerous . . . They'll beat you to a pulp . . .'

Her father didn't appear to hear. But watching from behind the curtain, with her mother sobbing at her side, she knew he had. She could see how he stiffened his body and walked more proudly. He had once been a 'Death's Head Hussar'; the Hussars were afraid of nothing, especially not the rabble that had collected in the waterside inns that lined the River Moselle in supposedly Catholic Trier.

'*Halt . . . Stehenbleiben, Jude!*' the command came from the door of the laundry opposite the synagogue which was already beginning to burn here and there. In the glowing cherry-red flames, Maertens, the SA leader from Trier, a feared brawler, who had once been sent to jail for stabbing a communist in a pub fight, stepped into the Himmeroderstrasse, his hand raised like a traffic cop halting the traffic.

Her father faltered for a moment. Everyone knew of Maertens' reputation. Then Dr Jacobsohn went on. There was a gasp from the mob. Maertens pulled a face and touched the ugly knife scar that ran the length of the left side of his face. He knew his reputation was at stake. He was being challenged by the damned old Yid. 'Stay where you are, if you know what's good for you,' he growled, clenching fists that looked like two steam shovels. 'Your medals won't save you.'

But instead of the murmur of support that he had expected from the mob that up to a few minutes ago was intent on burning down Wittlich's synagogue, there was a heavy silence. Maertens knew he had to act. If he waited much longer like this those damned two-timing 'March violets'* would be applauding the Yid. He stepped ever closer to Jacobsohn, barring his way, right fist raised threateningly.

The doctor didn't flinch. Indeed he didn't seem to see the raised fist. At their window, the girl had tensed, hardly breathing, eyes filled with horror with what surely had to come.

Slowly the doctor opened his mouth and said quite clearly, and seemingly unafraid, 'Please don't get in my way. I'm going to report a fire *personally*.' He indicated the flames starting to leap ever upwards around the Jewish church. 'It is essential that the volunteer fire brigade be turned out at once if the synagogue is to be saved.'

He stepped another pace forward. Now the confrontation between the doctor and the tough young Nazi thug had

---

*Name given to Germans who only joined the Nazi Party when Hitler won a second election in March 1933.

reached the critical phase, and the silent crowd knew it. Perhaps some of the older and more thoughtful of them realized too that this confrontation in the medieval Moselle township symbolized a much larger one between the harsh new regime of Adolf Hitler and the liberal one of the Jacobsohns and their kind.

Maertens lost his temper. He grabbed at the doctor's Iron Cross First Class. He grunted and tugged hard. The medal came away in his big paw. Not realizing just how stupid the move was, but carried away by a blinding rage, he flung it into the gutter. 'You damned castrated Jew!' he roared, his face purple, eyes bulging out of his head like those of a madman, 'You can't talk to us like that. We're—'

He got no further. Seeing the honoured decoration flung into the gutter like that enraged the mob. Almost instantly they broke into booing and whistling shrilly, crying, 'You swine, you can't do that . . . Shame on you . . . *Shame!*'

Maertens looked aghast. Even his own Trier thugs, bussed here purposely by the Party to show these backward small-town folk how they should deal with the Yids, were shouting at him. He staggered back a few paces. Again Dr Jacobsohn didn't appear to notice. Stiffly he bent and picked up the honoured decoration for bravery and pinned it back to his torn dress. Slowly, almost majestically, he went on his way, while behind him the flames leapt up higher and higher around the synagogue. He had won the first round.

The Party reacted swiftly. Two mornings later just after dawn, while Wittlich still slept, a thunderous knock came at the Jacobsohns' door and a harsh voice cried, '*Aufmachen . . . Los, aufmachen . . . Polizei . . .*'

It was the Gestapo. There was no mistaking the two heavy-set, middle-aged cops in their ankle-length leather coats that creaked every time they moved, and dark felt hats tugged down well over their foreheads so that it was hard to see the look in their eyes.

Hastily the flustered little maid summoned the doctor, while the daughter ran into her parents' bedroom to comfort her mother who was sobbing again and on the verge of hysterics.

The taller of the two showed his 'dog licence' and said to a suddenly subdued Doctor Jacobsohn, who knew he was dealing now with professionals and not ill-educated thugs like Maertens, 'We must ask you to come along with us, *Herr Doktor*. You can have ten minutes to pack the necessary: washbag, change of underwear—'

'What am I being arrested for?' her father interrupted, finding his voice at last.

The shorter of the two looked angry and as if he might make a sharp retort, but the other did not give him a chance to speak. He said, 'We're just carrying out orders. I cannot tell you any more, *Herr Doktor*.' He took the stump of the cheap cigar out of his mouth and added, 'Please do as you're told.'

'*No!*' His wife escaped her daughter's grip and ran to the head of the stairs, her blonde plaits flying, the tears streaming down her distraught face. 'Please don't take him. *Please*! He hasn't done anything.'

The cop with the cigar wasn't moved by her anguish, but politely, he said, '*Tut mir leid, Frau Doktor*, but your husband is a Jew and he has insulted an important Party member.'

At that moment she knew they were lost. Maertens was a lout and a bully, but over the years he had carried out a lot of the Party's dirty work in Catholic Trier, where normal Party members, afraid of the influence of the Church on the local populace, had maintained a low profile. The Party owed him a lot and now he was reclaiming that debt; he'd never forgive her father for the *Kristallnacht** stand-off. Her father was

---

*The 'night of the broken glass', when in revenge for the murder of a German diplomat by a Jew the Party ordered all synagogues to be burned down throughout the Reich.

103

doomed. Perhaps she and her mother, who wasn't Jewish, were too. Silently she watched as her father was taken away, his handcuffs hidden beneath his overcoat. He only looked back at them once, muttering softly, almost sadly, 'The world isn't all bad. There are good Germans, too . . . Remember that.' It was then that her mother screamed like some wild animal, caught in a trap and in extreme, unbearable pain. The next moment she had collapsed in a dead faint . . .

But the young girl was wrong. Her father wasn't doomed. He was indeed sent to a concentration camp at Neuengamme in the far north of Germany, but the Nazis didn't kill him. Indeed he was able to write to them and state he was in the camp hospital. The authorities even allowed them to send him a parcel once a month.

Naturally she and her mother began to suffer, although she was officially classified as a 'half Jew' or 'mixed race, first category' and was no longer allowed to cross the border to attend her language classes at the nearby French university of Metz. She was forced to take one of the few jobs allowed to Jews, while her mother sold little trinkets to buy their limited rations.

Slowly, as 1938 gave way to 1939, they started to overcome the shock of Doctor Jacobsohn's sudden arrest and their loss of status. Now they lived life from day to day, praying each new dawn that Father was still alive. Now their existence was dreary and isolated – their middle-class neighbours began to shun them – but it *was* an existence. At times they even started to hope again.

But in March of that year, with war clouds beginning to loom on the horizon and even more troops flooding into the border area and the local Adolf Hitler Kaserne, she was summoned to Berlin. At first she had been alarmed and frightened that it might have something to do with her father, but when she checked the address of the sender of the summons, in which there was a railway ticket, third class, coach 'reserved for Jews', she discovered that the Tirpitzufer was the headquarters of the German Navy. And for the life of her she couldn't understand what the German Navy wanted with a landlubber from the Moselle like herself and one who was a 'half Jew' to boot. She was soon to find out – to her cost. A new phase of her tragic life had commenced.

Two

S he walked, still puzzled at this strange summons to
Berlin, towards the massive grey block, the Tirpitzufer,
which lay between the local canal and the *Tiergarten*, and
passed into the low portico of the building which she would
come to know as the 'Foxes' Lair'. Inside there were
several sombre-faced men and women, some of whom were
obviously foreigners, and who were as equally puzzled as
she was.

At the desk, a stern-faced corporal of the *Wehrmacht*,
pistol holster at his brightly burnished belt, was examining
these people's ID cards and documents, checking them
against a list he had concealed on a shelf below his waist,
and when he was satisfied passing them to the Our Fathers,
the tiny wooden lifts with no doors that ran up and down
automatically.

When it came to her turn, he scrutinized her documents,
nodded his head in apparent approval and said, as he gave
her the number of the lift she should use, 'When you leave,
do not forget to put on your Jewish star, Fräulein Jacobsohn.
There might be a scene if the police stop you. And here we
don't want any trouble with the authorities. Good day.'

Puzzled even more she mounted the stairs to Lift 12,
wondering why the people in this obviously official building
with its armed military porter didn't want trouble with the
authorities.

In contrast to the quiet, even sombre, scene of the

106

entrance hall, the upper floor in which she now found herself bustled with activity. Telephones rang in the offices on both sides. There was the noisy clatter of teleprinters. Secretaries clacked back and forth on high heels, carrying their steno pads. High ranking officers of both army and navy passed to and fro, all immaculately uniformed and polished, engaged in deep, serious and sometimes whispered conversation. She felt completely out of place, a wallflower straight from the provinces, so dowdy and poorly dressed that no one deigned to take the slightest bit of notice of her. Later, she found out that wasn't true. She had been watched and shadowed ever since she had stepped off the train at the Lehrterbahnhof station.

It was only after she had wandered up and down the corridor a couple of times, feeling helpless and totally out of place, looking for office number twelve to which she had been ordered to report, and unable to find any number twelve, that a quiet voice behind her said, 'Fräulein Jacobsohn?'

She turned, startled. Facing her and smiling was a handsome young naval lieutenant, all blond hair and bright blue eyes, the perfect Aryan type, who to judge from the gleaming yellow lanyard hanging from his shoulder was some kind of aide or adjutant. 'Yes?'

The aide clicked his heels together and gave her a stiff little bow from his trim waist. '*Oberleutnant zur See Matz*,' he introduced himself. '*Zu Ihren Diensten.*'

She felt herself colouring red. He was such a handsome young man and she knew just what an ugly duckling she was – and a half Jew to boot. 'How do you do,' she heard herself say and stretched out her hand.

He didn't take it. Instead he said, '*Enchanté, M'selle.*' He extended one hand like a head waiter indicating a good table to a guest who tipped well, and added, '*L'Amiral vous attend.*'

It was only when she had started to follow him down the corridor that she realized with a start that this obviously German officer had spoken French to her.

He tapped politely at the top of yet another of the offices in the corridor, this one, however, with glazed pearl windows, and without waiting for an answer from within, turned to her and whispered, '*À bientôt, M'selle.*' And then he was gone as mysteriously as he had appeared, leaving her to open the door at the command of '*Herein.*'

At first sight the office in which she now found herself had appeared empty. It was a barren sort of a place, with little character. On the wall there was a Japanese painting of the devil and a photograph of a dachshund. On the opposite one there was a large map of Europe with none of the red and blue pins one might have expected from a place of this kind; perhaps it was meant simply as a wall covering, she had told herself. But on the uncluttered desk, there was a piece of cheap bric-a-brac that might have given her a clue to the nature of this place, if she had known more that March of 1939.

It was the familiar little statue of the three monkeys in their various postures, who hear, see, and speak no evil. It was, though she didn't know, the symbol of the *Abwehr*, chosen by the man who now rose from the floor where he had been feeding a fat, tail-wagging dachshund.

'*Guten Tag*, Fräulein Jacobsohn. My name is Canaris. I am glad you could come and see me. Please, sit down.' He indicated a straight-backed chair and took his seat opposite her on another equally straight-backed. Even then she noticed that the white-haired man in his shabby civilian suit (though she thought he was supposed to be an admiral) didn't offer her his hand in German fashion. Later, after September 1939 when he did, she realized just how flaccid his handshake was and how he always attempted to maintain a distance between himself and the people he had to deal with.

'I'm sure that you were surprised to receive our invitation to come to us in Berlin,' he commenced in a soft, somewhat tongue-tied manner, running his hand through his snow-white hair that made him look to be in his sixties, though, in reality, he was only in his late forties.

She stuttered something in reply, still wondering who this strange admiral was and what he wanted from her, a half-Jewess, whose father languished in a concentration camp and who had become an outcast in her own country.

'Now, Fräulein Jacobsohn,' he went on, 'I see that you have lived all your life in the border country between Germany and France, Luxembourg and Belgium. I see too that up to quite recently you were studying at the University of Metz in France. Why not in Germany?' Suddenly he gave her a sharp look and she realized that he was not at all the bumbling old fool that he appeared to be.

She did not tell him that her father had always insisted since she had left Wittlich's *Cusanusgymnasium* in 1937 that in view of the persecution of the Jews in the Reich, she must prepare for a life abroad; English and French and university education in nearby France might well prepare her for that. Instead she answered, 'My father always believed in a broad education—'

He chuckled and interrupted her with an icy: 'You mean your father thought that if you were forced to depart hastily from Germany, probably with diamonds in your gullet and gold bars hidden in the heels of your shoes, you could make another life abroad.' He noted the look of alarm in her dark eyes and his tone changed immediately. 'Don't worry, my dear,' he said gently, 'I know and understand these things. And by the way, you'd never get away with swallowing diamonds. The Gestapo always give a dose of castor oil to your people trying to leave legally. It's crude but effective. Better find some professional Belgian smuggler to take you through the woods of the Eifel Forest. Much more effective.'

Again his tone changed. 'But Fräulein, let us not waste any more time. I am going to put a proposition to you.'

'What kind of propostion?' she asked warily. For now she had realized that she was dealing, not only with a cunning man, but also a dangerous one.

'Espionage. To work for me,' he answered bluntly, assessing her with his cunning gaze.

'*For Germany*?' she blurted out.

'No – to save your father's life! Let me put it this way. You do what I say – and I promise you will be well rewarded for work for my *Abwehr* – and your father's life will be safe. I shall arrange that with Gestapo Mueller, the head of the Berlin Gestapo. If you are not willing to do so . . .' He shrugged carelessly and left the rest of his sentence unsaid.

Thus she had been blackmailed into what she would learn to call 'the war in the shadows': a secret world of dealing and double-dealing, where treachery was the name of the game and traitors disappeared mysteriously and without trace if they were found out.

It wasn't a nice world, but in the months to come, Rachel Jacobsohn soon was to realize that the world wasn't nice and probably never had been nice. Indeed she found her world, already put seriously out of joint by the cruel arrest of her adored father, was now turned upside down. She learned to be suspicious all the time, furtive, ready at a moment's notice to melt into the shadows, to avoid the slightest confrontation, even one between herself and a cafe waiter, for instance, when she suspected he had fiddled her bill.

At first Father Christmas, as she, too, had learned to call Canaris, the head of the *Abwehr* (behind his back naturally), had given her easy assignments. She was to check the Luxembourgers' defences around the River Moselle where that tiny principality bordered the Reich. That had been easy. The Luxembourgers had none. From there she was switched back to France. She was given back her student papers, precious French currency and a special pass which enabled her to cross back and forth between Germany and France without hindrance from the German border police, who were now all members of the SS. Here her task was to assess the strength of the French defences around Sedan, the scene of the famous German victory of 1870 which had forced France to surrender during the Franco-Prussian War. Here, where the celebrated French Maginot Line came to a virtual end, she discovered the French had been very slack. Their defences there were weak.

Rachel Jacobsohn was no fool. It didn't take her long to work out why she was being used in these border assignments. The *Abwehr* was preparing the ground for a German Army attack westwards. Sooner or later the *Wehrmacht* would launch an offensive against France, probably through such weak spots as Luxembourg and Sedan, and thus avoiding a frontal assault on the allegedly impregnable French Maginot Line.

When Hitler attacked Poland on August 31st, 1939, she thought she might have been wrong in her assessment. The Nazis were moving eastwards, preparing perhaps to attack the hated communists in Russia. Father Christmas soon enlightened her that the war on Poland was just a preliminary to a much larger one with the Franco-British alliance in the west. She was now to go to Flanders in Belgium, where many of the Dutch-speaking and anti-French population apparently would welcome 'liberation from the yoke of their fellow French-speaking Belgians by the Führer'. There her task would be to use these people to obtain various types of uniform for the *Abwehr*'s own special forces. Father Christmas didn't tell her why, but she guessed the reason. The *Abwehr* was planning some sort of Trojan Horse operation in front of the *Wehrmacht*'s assault divisions, for which they would need enemy uniforms.

111

Thus it was that she first met Giselle of the Dunkirk brothel, though in the winter of 1939/40 she wasn't called Giselle, she wasn't blonde and she didn't run a brothel in Dunkirk.

Instead she was mousy brown, her face permanently set in a look of wary suspicion, and was inclined to wear men's suits after her teaching work at the local Flemish *anthenée* was over. It was clear, too, that Minvrouw van Donk, as was Giselle's real name, didn't like her from the very start, perhaps, she told herself, because the Flemish woman guessed she was Jewish and because she shared the same racial prejudices as the Nazis for whom she worked.

Still, she co-operated loyally enough. Together they obtained, through bribery, theft and active support of other Flemings in the administration who believed in a 'Free Flanders', every type of Belgian uniform imaginable: from that of the Belgian frontier guards down to (for some inexplicable reason) those of Brussels tram conductors.

Father Christmas was very pleased with them. Indeed, he came to visit the heads of the clandestine Flemish organization and his German representative Rachel Jacobsohn, and congratulated them on their 'sterling work'. Afterwards, he invited her to have tea with him at a discreet little English tearoom in Bruges where the meeting had taken place to brief her on further developments.

As they sipped their tea and ate the too-sweet Belgian tarts and creamcakes (Father Christmas had a decidedly sweet tooth), he gave her what news he had of her father. He was well. He was working in a medical orderly capacity in the concentration camp's 'hospital' and writing regularly each month to her mother back in Wittlich, who was now receiving a small allowance from the *Abwehr*, enough at least to keep her head above water.

For a while they chatted about Belgium, while he cast furtive glances at her when he thought she wasn't looking at him, as if he were seeing her for the very first time. She saw the looks. For by now she had trained herself to observe certain people of whom she was suspicious. She'd view their reflection in a shop window or a mirror on the wall. It had become part and parcel of the clandestine illegal life she was now leading as a German agent against her will.

But why was Canaris attempting to size her up like this? Surely he had to know her weaknesses and strengths by now? What was the white-haired spymaster, who had been in the 'great game', as it was called, since World War One, up to?

It was just when she thought that he was ready to leave to catch his train back to Brussels and from there to the German border at Aachen, that he revealed what was on his mind and what had occasioned this private meeting with her.

'Fräulein Jacobsohn,' he said slowly, as if he were con-sidering his words carefully, 'I would like you to take part in one final mission. It will be difficult, very difficult for you – I shall tell you that in advance. But if you help to make this mission a success, I will offer you something – and you have my word of honour as a gentleman and a German officer that I will not renegade on what I can promise you now.'

He paused and let his words sink in. She felt a sense of mixed apprehension and hope. Abruptly her hands began to tremble nervously. 'Does it concern my father?' she asked.

Father Christmas gave her a hint of a smile. 'You are a clever girl, Fräulein Jacobsohn. That's why I have really selected you. You have learned when you are faced with powerful and superior forces, it is no use attempting to fight against them. One must go with the current and survive. A very few people learn that in this life. But I digress.' He cleared his throat, as if he were about to make a public speech. 'You see, Fräulein van Donk is about to set up a certain establishment in France. You won't, as a well-bred young lady, particularly like her new establishment, but probably when I tell you that I want you to go with her, you'll say to yourself, "Ah-ah, the old fool is giving me the chance to betray him and turn van Donk over to the French".' He smiled at her, but there was no answering warmth in his dark secretive eyes. 'But of course, when you have heard my offer, you won't do anything of the sort. You see, Fräulein, carry out this mission and your father goes free. Not only that, *mein liebes Fräulein*, your father, you and your mother will be given passes and sufficient money to leave the Reich and take yourselves to Switzerland. From there, you can abandon Europe altogether. Perhaps America? All you people have rich relatives in the United States, I believe.'

It was a bad tactical mistake, that 'all you people', but Father Christmas didn't seem to notice it and she didn't care. For her heart was racing suddenly with a new-found hope and joy. Her father freed, the family reunited, able to escape from Germany to that neutral base of Switzerland, from whence they might be able to leave a hateful, decadent, cruel old Europe for ever. 'What is the task, sir?' she asked, trying to keep her voice from showing too much enthusiasm.

'This. Van Donk is to open – er – a bordello in Dunkirk – the port is one of the Tommies' major ports and staging posts in France. There will be plenty ot troops stationed there or passing through, and like all young men, they will need the sexual services of women.' The old Admiral actually blushed and lowered his gaze momentarily. 'They will prove an invaluable source of information for us.'

She looked puzzled. 'And my role, sir?'

'You will watch van Donk. These Flemings are like us in many ways, Germanic, nationalist and hard working. But they are peasants and they have all the rural defects of the peasants. In other words, she has to be watched and you will do the watching, Fräulein Jacobsohn.' The white-haired spymaster paused, as if he were hesitating about how to

114

phrase what he was to say next. 'You know now what is at stake for you personally?'

She nodded.

'You know, too, what your mission is, one that you must always keep secret from the good van Donk, until, quite frankly, we don't need the van Donks of this world and Germany is supreme in Europe. But let me say this . . . perhaps regard it as a warning, eh? She and her kind are dangerous people when roused – irrational.'

'How do you mean, sir?'

Father Christmas didn't appear to hear her question. 'So take care, my dear Fräulein Jacobsohn.' There was a sudden warmth in his voice which puzzled her as so many of the little spymaster's actions puzzled those who knew him, before his Führer finally had him strung up by a length of chicken wire and strangled to death – slowly. 'Goodbye Fräulein, I doubt if we shall meet again.'

And with that he was gone, a seemingly old man in a shabby suit whom one wouldn't give a second glance. He left her more puzzled than ever.

Three

The move from Belgium to wartime France and the waterfront brothel at Dunkirk transformed the ex-schoolteacher and nationalist van Donk. She gave up wearing mannish clothing, including men's ties, and turned herself into the popular image of a brothel-keeper: blowsy, blonde (now she dyed her hair a bright yellow), and big-hearted. Well might she water the champagne she served her 'clients', but she always had a welcome, even for the humblest British private, who had scraped a couple of weeks pay together to patronize her establishment. She had even learned some basic English to make them feel at home before they went upstairs, clutching their little towels and contraceptives for a 'little jig-jig'.

Naturally she favoured officers and those of the merchant ships and freighters who brought supplies and troops across for the British Expeditionary Force which was stationed up between Dunkirk and the Belgian frontier. For Father Christmas was obviously anxious to find out the BEF's strength and its intentions, once the German Panzer armies attacked Belgium and Luxembourg. But in that winter of the phoney war of 1939/40, it seemed the Tommies were engaged solely in building fortifications along France's frontier with neutral Belgium, and had no obvious intention of attacking anywhere, certainly not against the territory of the Reich.

In her job of the brothel's bookkeeper and interpreter –

116

when needed, for none of the girls spoke much English save the few key words required in their profession: 'How much?' . . . 'You go upstairs with me?' . . . 'You have french letter, soldier?' . . . and the like – she was to keep her ears open for any piece of secret information that the English might reveal in their cups. She was also to note and report upon the divisional and corps signs of the twelve British divisions which now made up their army in France.

It was busy and relatively easy work, but she was happy to do it, for it kept her apart from the girls that Madame Giselle had recruited locally. They were the riff-raff of the port, the type who till recently had catered for the North Africans, who made up most of the lower decks of the French freighters which had visited Dunkirk. The girls, hardly one of whom was under the age of thirty-five, were raddled hussies, who seemed to spend their free time while they were waiting for clients lolling around in the shabby cheap underwear, scratching their pubic hair, smoking and drinking vermouth, and in the case of those who could read, leafing in a bored fashion through cheap paperback novelettes. All save the redhead, Anna, whom she had brought with her from Bruges and who was a Fleming like Madame Giselle.

The redhead, Anna, made it quite clear that she didn't like the 'little Yid', as she called Rachel behind her back, 'with her frigging fancy ways and fancy talk . . . she ought to be dancing the mattress polka four or five times like we do, then she'd know what the real frigging world's about.' And she would spit contemptuously on the floor, or if she happened to be on the chamberpot at the time (and all of the girls had bladder complaints which kept them running to the privy all the time), she'd give a noisy, long, insulting fart, as a sign of how deep her contempt was for the German girl.

Rachel had made it her policy to keep out of Anna's way, because she knew the redhead was Madame Giselle's

117

favourite. At first she had been unable to understand their relationship. In the early afternoons, while the girls lazed and chatted or napped after a heavy French lunch, the two of them would retire to Madame Giselle's room while she watched over the shop below. From her position at the till, she'd hear them lock the door. That would be followed by the clink of glasses and, at first, whispered conversation and giggles. Now and again, Madame would send the redhead down for another bottle of the English rum that they favoured. Anna would clatter down the stairs, her hair tousled, her tough face suddenly foolish and even girlish, her naked body occasionally glanced beneath the dressing gown she put on for such occasions. There'd be more drinking followed this time by shrill drunken laughter. Thereafter a strange abrupt silence, sometimes broken by a hectic gasping and panting like someone in the throes of an asthma attack.

It was only later as 1939 gave way to 1940 that she realized what the two of them were doing. It was the girls who really enlightened her in that crude manner of theirs.

One afternoon when Madame Giselle and Anna were, as usual, locked in the former's bedroom getting steadily drunk, Bernice came down the stairs to the shop for a drink. As always she was dressed in her high-heeled laced boots and fading corset, tugging her whip behind her, as if it weighed a ton. Rachel had told herself that if her father had been asked to have a look at the hard-faced blonde whore, he would state without hesitation that she was suffering from 'galloping consumption'.

Bernice had sat herself wearily on one of the hard-backed chairs and said, panting a little with the effort of coming down the stairs, 'Give me a beer, *cherie*. That last sailor was just too much. Now my mouth feels dry as dust, even with all that lubrication, if you know what I mean?' She winked in a tired way.

118

Rachel Jacobsohn had understod. She'd learned a lot about the perverted pleasures of young men – and old ones, too – over the last few weeks. She'd blushed and handed over an open bottle of Jupiter beer. The blonde had taken it and swallowed a great gulp greedily. Above their heads the springs of Madame Giselle's bed had begun to squeak alarmingly.

Bernice wiped her wet lips with the back of her hand and with a malicious grin she'd said, 'The two Flemish cows are at it again, I hear. *Mon Dieu, les sales cons*, you'd think with all the cock that comes into this frigging place, they wouldn't want that as well, wouldn't you?'

'Want what?' she had asked innocently.

Bernice had looked at her, as if she were some kind of alien. She stretched out her skinny hands and sneered, 'That much hard rubber.'

Rachel Jacobsohn had an uncertain idea, a frightening, disgusting one, of what the whore meant, but she was not sure at all. She'd stuttered, 'Rubber . . . I don't understand, Bernice.'

The whore had looked at her. 'Where you been all your life?' she'd demanded. 'Hasn't the penny dropped yet*?'

Above them the bedsprings were creaking mightily now and the sound of hectic panting was all too clear.

'You mean they're a little strange, Bernice?' She'd felt herself flushing a deep red even as she uttered the words.

'A *little strange*!' the whore had exploded. 'Holy straw sack! You can't get no stranger than them two.' And with that, she'd downed the rest of her beer in one gulp and tottered upstairs, breathing hard with the effort, as if she were climbing the North Face of the Eiger. But at the top, clutching her side, her raddled withered breasts threatening to fall out of the tight corset as she bent to gather her breath,

---

*In German: *'Ist der Groschen nicht gefallen?'* Transl.

she'd wheezed, 'Take my advice, and don't be . . . alone with either of that pair . . . in the same room . . .' Then she was gone.

It was two nights before the Flemings murdered the young English signals corporal that she learned – to her cost – just how timely that warning had been.

It was a quiet Wednesday. Apparently the English indulged in sport on Wednesday afternoons, war or no war. They went for runs, they played their football and they jumped up and down energetically in their overlong, rather ridiculous navy-blue shorts. The result was that they were too worn out to indulge in another more interesting form of exercise in Madame Giselle's establishment. As a result, they had few customers and Madame Giselle's afternoon session with the redhead had gone on well into the evening, the two of them consuming over a bottle of the rotgut sailors' rum they preferred. By seven that evening, for reasons known only to themselves, they were arguing loudly and in the end the redhead staggered out of Madame's bedroom, locked herself in her own tiny and filthy room and fell asleep weeping miserably.

Not Madame Giselle. Seemingly she had not been satis-fied, and Rachel, who had taken advantage of the slackness of their business and who had retired to her cubbyhole to write her monthly letter to her father, was shocked out of her reverie by a loud hammering on her door and Madame Giselle demanding thickly, 'Open this door, girl, if you know what's good for you . . . at once, do you hear!'

For a moment she panicked. She froze, unable to react. She knew that Madame Giselle reported directly to Father Christmas through channels she kept open with her native Flanders. Her father's fate, and probably her mother's too, back in Wittlich, depended on whether or not the gross per-verted Flemish mare reported favourably on her to Berlin.

So she pulled herself together by a sheer effort of naked will power, forcing herself to say in a neutral sort of a voice, 'One moment, Madame . . . I'm opening the door.'

'Better be damned quick!' Madame Giselle thundered.

She opened the bolt and staggered back, shocked and at the same time very frightened. Instinctively her hands flew to her mouth to prevent herself from crying out loud and alerting the other girls.

Madame Giselle was standing there, totally naked, swaying drunkenly, her face flushed and angry. But it wasn't the Flemish woman's gross nakedness that made her reel back. It was the obscene instrument, strapped to her hairy loins, which shocked her beyond all measure.

It was made of leather and rubber, and jutted out in front of her and wobbled obscenely every time the drunken brothel-keeper swayed. She leered now at Rachel and looked down at the artifical penis. 'You are impressed, eh?' She rubbed the end of the monstrous instrument for an instant. 'It probably frightens you a bit, eh. Don't worry. After the first time you'll get to like it. They all do. In the end you'll be begging for it.' She licked her thick red lips, the saliva drooling down her chin in anticipation. 'After I've done with them, girl, I can tell you,' she boasted, 'they'll never want another man . . . Now, let's not waste time. It's cold out here in the corridor.' She shuddered dramatically and every part of her fat gross body wobbled disgustingly. She made a pace forward.

Hastily, frightened out of her mind, she had grabbed the door and held it tightly to bar Madame Giselle from entering. 'No,' she said firmly, iron in her voice suddenly, 'you're not coming in, Madame.'

'*What!*' she exploded, her piglike little eyes red with rage. 'How dare you speak to me like that, you little Yid.'

Rachel had never felt herself so cool, so in charge of a

situation. 'You heard what I said, Madame. You're not coming in. I don't—'

She gasped and held on to the door just in time as the Flemish woman put her full weight against the door and attempted to thrust her back. At any other time, the scene would have seemed grotesquely funny, even absurd: a fat Flemish woman, wearing an artificial penis and playing at being a man, being confronted by a skinny dark-eyed girl, who was half her size. But not now. For Rachel knew that it was not merely a matter of her protecting her body from the other woman's perverted lusts, but also that her parents' lives were perhaps at stake.

But her determination had paid off. Suddenly Madame Giselle gave in. Perhaps she simply had had too much to drink and hadn't the stamina to keep up the fight. She ceased trying to force the door, the artificial penis slipping now and seeming to droop like a real one might after an unsuccessful encounter. But she wasn't altogether finished with Rachel, whose heart was now beating frantically like a trip hammer. 'You'll regret this, my girl,' she said as she turned ready to waddle back to her own room. 'For me, you will be just like the rest – a common whore, just about good enough to service one of those dirty English Tommies. And you know what will happen if you don't do as I say, don't you . . .'

With that she went, leaving that terrible threat hanging over Rachel's head for the rest of that awful day and far into the night, so that she tossed and turned sleeplessly, unable to find peace. She knew that Madame Giselle would carry out her threat. She would force her to line up with the rest like a bunch of animals at a county fair being auctioned off to the highest bidder, and she would have to go along with it, if she wanted her father to live. In the end she cried herself to sleep, moaning in her nightmare, 'Oh God, help me . . . what am I to do? *God help me!*'

But God wasn't listening that night.

Four

S he had felt so ashamed at first. Indeed, when Madame
Giselle had told her with a sneer, 'You're on duty
tonight, Jewess,' her head had whirled and she had almost
fainted. It had become even worse when the brothel-keeper
had flung the transparent black shift at her, commanding,
'You'll wear that, though God only knows who'd want to
see those scraggy little tits of yours.'

Then she had told herself that she had to refuse. With luck
she'd run from the house and tell the French authorities what
she knew of this dreadful house and its use as an espionage
centre for the German enemy.

A moment later reason had reasserted itself. She couldn't
condemn her father in Neuengamme Concentration Camp
to die just like that. Besides, would they let her escape
from the shabby waterfront house? After all, she knew too
much. Somehow she felt they wouldn't; she'd never leave
the place alive.

In the end she had accepted her fate; and it had not turned
out to be as dreadful as she had anticipated. The young
corporal had actually been more shy and embarrassed than
she; the whole business had been done and over in a matter
of minutes. She had watched him as she washed herself in
the little bedroom sink and she had told herself he was a
mere boy. She hoped that he had some pleasure from her
amateurish and reluctant efforts.

It had been just about then that she had heard the voices

outside: male voices talking in that crude guttural Flemish which she had learned to understand in the last few months. She had been hardly able to conceal her shock. They were going to kill the two Tommies. For one brief instant she had not known what to do. Should she allow the murder to take place and thus save her father? Or should she warn him? Then it had come to her; there was another way out. The way the whores used when the police raided the place to show higher authority they were up to their job; though in fact they routinely accepted bribes from Madame Giselle to look the other way. The fact that the next moment the radio had been turned on louder below convinced her that she must act and save the young Tommy. The raised volume indicated that the sound was going to be used to drown out any noise the victims might make.

It was then that she had alerted the corporal to the mortal danger in which he now found himself. But it had been all in vain. Half an hour after he had fled the knocking shop, the two hulking Flemings in their leather coats and dark felt hats had dragged the body back into the brothel.

The young English corporal had been stripped (it was only much later that she found out why). Now he lay in all his pale-white nakedness on the floor, his manhood shrivelled and no longer of importance. Brutally, one of the big Flemings turned him over with the tip of his boot. She and the other whores gathered to see the spectacle and gasped. The back of the boy's head had been blown away. Now, where the dark hair had covered his skull, there was a gory red mess through which the bone shone like polished ivory.

Madame Giselle was totally unmoved by the ghastly sight. She said, 'Don't mess up the shitting floor, you damned fools. Why bring him back here? Get him into the canal. Wait.' She held up her hand to halt them. 'Where's the other one? The little one with the false teeth.'

The Fleming men shrugged.

Angrily she snapped, '*Je kunt wel gaan. Ik heb je vanavond niet meer nodig.*'

Hastily they picked up the body and went out, as if they couldn't get out of the place and away from Madame Giselle's sharp tongue soon enough.

Madame Giselle frowned. 'Not a word of this to anyone,' she warned the whores. '*Hoor je dat*?' She repeated her warning in French to the ones who weren't Flemings.

The whores mumbled their assent in the same instant that the missing whore reappeared and said, 'He wanted a drink across the road and when I said I couldn't, he dragged me . . .'

But by then Rachel Jacobsohn had not been listening any longer. She knew now that she was in grave danger, but she couldn't let the others, especially Madame Giselle, know that she was aware of her situation. Somehow or other she had to get out of the waterfront brothel without arousing the big Flemish mare's suspicions, which could only mean her father's death. But how. *HOW*?

It was fortunate that at that time she got her period which meant she wouldn't be able to service the Tommies who mostly frequented the place. She was exceedingly grateful for her period and for the time it gave her back in the shop below to dwell on her problem, though Madame Giselle did sneer, 'You've got other holes haven't you, Jewess? Those Tommies have dirty habits as it is. They're not so particular.' But she had ignored the comment, lowering her head and her eyes which were full of bitter hate for the 'Flemish mare', as she now called her to herself.

But although she thought long and hard about the problem she had set herself, knowing that time was against her (her periods would be over soon), she could come to no solution. But for once, as she saw it at the time, luck was on her side.

On that May 10th, 1940 when it all began, the whores in Giselle's establishment found that no single client turned up from the half a million strong British Army in France – there was a drunken lascar, who said he was British, from one of the freighters, but he was found not to have a single penny, only able to offer them a bunch of green bananas, which he believed was a great delicacy in France.

The absence of the missing khaki customers was solved later on that same day. The Belgian *passeur*, or illegal 'front runner', arrived on his motorbike from his native country, which had been invaded that morning, to report to Madame Giselle and to bring the newest orders from Father Christmas.

The Germans had finally attacked westwards. Both Luxembourg and Belgium had been invaded. The German juggernaut was heading for France. According to the white-haired spymaster, the objective of the assault was firstly the French coast and then Paris. No further details were given. Naturally, Father Christmas being Father Christmas didn't even trust his own spies. However he did inform the Flemish mare that he needed a new contact in England; something had gone wrong there. He didn't specify what.

'You're going,' Madame Giselle told Rachel that very same night, as outside on the cobbled quayside the steady tramp of the reinforcements for the front went on and on. 'You're the only one who speaks good English. Like all Jews,' she added, unable to resist a final sneer, 'you speak languages because you can live anywhere and are at home *nowhere*. Now get your pathetic bits and pieces together and prepare to leave on the midnight tide. I'll tell you about the contact in Dover afterwards.'

At first the news had excited Rachel; she was getting away from the dreadful brothel and its lesbian owner. Then she was assailed by doubts. Was Madame Giselle really sending her to England or was this leaving 'on the midnight tide' just a convenient means of getting her down to the docks – and perhaps a watery grave? Such things did happen in Dunkirk. She knew that by now . . .

'You'll go down into the anchor locker,' the purser had whispered as they had crouched in the shadow cast by the rusty old tub's neglected superstructure. 'It'll be crowded, but you're only a slip of a girl.' He spat the remainder of the Gauloise glued to his bottom lip over the side carelessly, as if he didn't care whether *poilu* lounging against a winch half a dozen metres away spotted them or not. But then, she told herself, it seemed that every Frenchman she had ever met could be bought if the price were right. Perhaps the sentry had been bribed to look the other way as well.

She had looked down the dark pit into which the great rusty anchor chain would be wound once the anchor had been raised, and shuddered. 'Is it safe?' she'd asked in a whisper.

'God bless you, *M'selle*,' the purser, who smelled of garlic and cognac, had chuckled and reaching out as if to reassure her had touched her breast and added, '*Bien sûr*.' He'd let his hand rest on her left breast, as if he were steadying her. 'We use the anchor locker all the time for – er – business. Once the *rostbifs*' – he meant the English customs – 'have finished their usual business, we'll have you out like greased lightning. *Merde*,' he'd added with a curse, 'why don't they take a little tip like our brave French customs and save themselves all that silly paperwork.' He shook his head, as if he couldn't understand by the best will in the world, the stupidity of the English.

Carefully she had guided his hand, which was reaching for her nipple, away from her breast, saying, 'All right, I suppose I have to do it.'

'Don't worry,' he'd replied, in no way upset, 'I'll see you get some sandwiches – and a bucket, just in case—'

'I understand,' she'd cut him off sharply. Then taking a

deep breath she had commencing climbing down the wet and very slippery rungs of the ladder that led into the darkness.

Thus she came to Dover, wet, cold and somewhat shaky, yet at the same relieved. She was free of Dunkirk and all the things that went on there, she'd told herself, as she crouched in the semi-darkness, waiting to be released from the chain locker. Faintly she'd heard cheerful voices somewhere on the quay outside where the freighter had docked. Someone was whistling happily and a hoarse male voice was chanting, *'There was jam, jam mixed up with the ham in the quartermaster's stores . . . My eyes are dim . . . I cannot see . . . I have not brought my specs with* me *. . .'*

To Rachel, the persecuted Jewess and spy against her will, it seemed the English in their own country were a happy people despite what was happening in France. There, the workers were surly, bad-tempered and apparently against the world just for the sake of being against it. Here, she thought, she might be able to work something out that would relieve her of the terrible guilty burden of spying for a regime she hated, and save her father at the same time. Suddenly she felt happy, the first time for a very long, long time.

Her happiness had been short-lived. Abruptly she was startled by the sound of someone tapping, perhaps with a spanner, against the top of the chain locker. It was some kind of signal. *'Oui, qui est la?'* she demanded, thinking it was the purser.

The answer came in flawless North German, *'Ich bin es . . . deine Komtaktperson. Hor mir gut zu, Rachel.'*

There followed a swift series of instructions, rapped out in a hoarse hushed tone, as if the unspoken speaker above were afraid he might be discovered at any moment and wanted to be off before that happened.

'Ja . . . ja,' she kept repeating, feeling a sudden sense of let-down that she was being forced into the network

once more against her will. 'But who are you?' she asked when the speaker, who sounded young and educated to judge from his use of the language, was finished with his hurried orders.

'You don't need to know that,' came the reply. 'The less you know, Rachel, the better. Don't worry, you'll be supplied with plenty of money and looked after. The Admiral has told me about you and I don't mind working with Jews one bit. Remember that you must never try to contact me . . . I shall contact *you*.' And with that he had gone.

Half an hour later, the purser had released her, and carrying a large bundle as if she were one of the crew of the old tub, she had stepped on English soil for the very first time. It was raining.

PART FOUR:
THE NET CLOSES IN

One

'Here the bastard comes again,' the wounded gunner cried angrily as the dark red blood started pouring down his wounded arm. 'Shit, I can't get the mag on!'

'Here, let me,' Mackenzie yelled against the howl of the Heinkel's twin engines, as the plane's black and sinister shape came skimming over Dover's sea wall, heading straight for the sinking ferry and the men splashing and spluttering in the harbour, yelling for help.

Dalby lowered the wounded gunner to the bullet-chipped jetty and thrust another round magazine of ammunition at his assistant, as he swung the old-fashioned Lewis round on its tripod to meet the renewed challenge.

In one and the same moment, the young sergeant rammed home the magazine, cocked the weapon and started firing. A stream of white tracer raced towards the Heinkel in a lethal morse. A vicious splatter of red came from the Heinkel, as it took up the challenge. Now the twin-engined German fighter-bomber was so low that its prop wash-lashed and thrashed the water into a vicious white-topped fury.

Swinging the heavy old-fashioned machine gun from side to side, Mackenzie peppered the diving Heinkel. Pieces of it, ripped from the fuselage, fell like metallic leaves. The cockpit was hit. The pilot's goggled head disappeared behind the gleaming spiderweb of plexiglas. Still he came on. It was as if he were concentrating totally on wiping out this puny David who was attempting to stop him

133

massacring the frantic survivors in the water of the harbour.

But luck was on Mackenzie's side. Suddenly black smoke started to stream from the Heinkel's port engine. The prop faltered and fell silent. The Heinkel tilted to starboard. Frantically the almost blinded German pilot attempted to hold her. In vain. He lost control. Mackenzie caught one last fleeting glimpse of the German throwing up his hands in front of his face in absolute despair. Then he was soaring over their heads at mast height. Next moment the Heinkel crumpled into the cliff beyond. In a great ball of cherry-red flame it exploded and disintegrated. Bits and pieces of torn rended metal tumbled down the chalk face in the loud echoing silence which followed.

Then Mackenzie and Dalby forgot the downed plane. They continued helping the others to pull out the dead and those still alive from the mess around the sinking ferry. It was a terrible task – and sight. For the first time Sergeant Mackenzie, the former doctoral candidate and scholar, knew what real war was. There were no clean deaths here, as portrayed in the Hollywood films: noble commanders shot through the heart with no blood visible; men dying with a smile on their faces and one last word of encouragement for their brave comrades.

Here death was obscene, disgusting. A sailor, his head jammed in a locker, perhaps choked to death, kneeling as if in prayer as he bobbed up and down on the wavelots. A redheaded woman, totally naked, her stomach ripped open, trailing her intestines like ugly grey eels in the water behind her. An old soldier by the look of him, his skinny nut-brown arm bearing a tattoo of a swallow and the legend 'Mother' written on a fading blue scroll – a mother he'd never see again.

'God Almighty, sir!' he gasped to Dalby as the two of them hauled a panting soldier who was still holding on to his rifle, as if his life depended on it, on to the jetty where he collapsed like a gasping stranded fish. 'This is hell!'

Dalby said grimly, 'You'll see worse, Mac, before this little lot is over, I'll be bound. Give me a hand with that young squaddie over there . . . she's going down fast.

The ferry was. The ship's bow was rising in the water, her screws still churning it into a white fury, fringed with the brown scum of the harbour. Frantically those who were still alive and close to the sinking ship exerted the last of their strength to get away while there was still a chance. Those who couldn't swim dog-paddled or thrashed the water, heads raised high above its level, spluttering and shouting for help. Others who could swim pushed aside those who attempted to cling on to them and drag them down. Now it was every man for himself.

But the rescuers were out in force, fishing for the closest survivors with boathooks. Others, more plucky, had dropped over the jetty into the water and were attempting to drag the exhausted survivors, careful to fend them off with hard blows if they tried to get a firm hold of them. Slowly, now the danger of air attack was temporarily over, order was being restored and as the stricken ferry finally went under, accompanied by the obscene belches of the trapped air in bubbles exploding in a series of what seemed like giant farts, those who would live were being stretched out on the jetty, being covered with blankets, handed lit cigarettes, while the NAAFI tea trolleys were being hurried to dish out that universal English panacea for all ailments – tca!

For a while Dalby and his young sergeant seemed dazed. They slumped against a derrick in a numbed way, as if they were not aware of the joy mixed up with the misery all around them. They stared at the drifting human flotsam in the harbour, entangled in the wreckage of the ferry, as if they might be watching the newsreel of some tragedy in the local cinema which had no relevance to their lives.

135

Finally Dalby tossed his cigarette end into the dirty water below and said tonelessly, 'Let's see if we can scrounge a cup of tea from the NAAFI lady, then we'll get back to the office –' he gave a wintry smile – 'and that bloody problem of ours.'

Mackenzie nodded his agreement, feeling he knew more about Dalby's and his generation's attitude now that he had seen the tragedy of the ferry. They had witnessed some terrible things in their lives; now obviously it was his turn in this new shooting war. Idly he wondered if he would become so hard and cynical as Dalby was? But he could find no answer to that question.

In single file they threaded their way through the wounded lying on the jetty waiting for medical attention, while other survivors huddled in brown army blankets and cradled their hands round jam jars of hot tea – the NAAFI had run out of mugs – their heads wreathed in steam, savouring the warmth. Somewhere among the stretchers a weak, frightened voice was sobbing, 'Don't tell me I'm blind, doctor . . . please don't say that, sir.' Mackenzie forced himself not to look in that particular direction. He felt he had seen enough this day.

Ahead of him, Major Dalby had turned down an offer of the tea-filled jam jar. He was obviously old school enough to insist on something better as an officer. Instead he was pouring himself a whisky from his silver flask, saying over his shoulder, 'Get yourself some char, Sergeant. You can have a shot of this, if you wish.'

'Thank you, sir,' Mackenzie answered in the same instant as the girl who was serving tea turned, a jam jar ready in her hand, her dark face suffused with sorrow, the tears still wet on her thin cheeks. But at that particular moment, Staff Sergeant Mackenzie didn't see the sorrowful face or the tear-stained cheeks caused by the terrible events which had just taken place in the harbour.

Instead he saw her *Hahnenkamm*, that peculiar German hairstyle, the cockscomb, which he had been looking for for days now. '*Grösser Gott!*' he exclaimed in German, caught totally by surprise. '*Sie sind's!*'

Rachel Jacobsohn knew it was over. Even as she dropped the jam jar, which shattered into myriad fragments at her feet on the wet jetty, she felt a sense of overwhelming relief that it was over, come what may. She could tell her story at last . . .

A hundred yards or so away, the Old Sweat, still wrappped in a blanket, but wearing a fine pair of brown boots that he had stolen from a dead officer sprawled on the jetty with the rest, was posing happily for the photographers of the *Picture Post* and the *Daily Mirror*. Behind him in the khaki-clad mass at the station barrier, a bugler was playing 'Land of Hope and Glory' while a drunken major in the Pay Corps was declaiming, '*And gentlemen in England now abed, Shall think themselves accurs'd they were not here: And hold their manhood cheap whiles any speaks, That fought with us upon St Crispin's Day.*'

But it was the Old Sweat who held centre stage as far as the popular press was concerned. He told the admiring reporters the story 'the way it was', while the photographers circled him with their tripod cameras clicking away all the time. 'Bloody marvellous!' the man from the *Daily Mirror* exclaimed out loud, as the Old Sweat raised his tea mug yet once again as if in toast to some great victory for the benefit of the photographers. Even without his false teeth which he had lost in the water, he looked the epitome of the English Tommy. 'We ain't downhearted,' he lisped, 'are we, mates? Old 'Itler will have ter get up earlier in the morning to do in the British Empire.'

Even as he said the words, the man from the *Mirror* told himself that 'bloody marvellous' would make a terrific caption under the Old Sweat's triumphant photo. It'd put the

Dunkirk business into perspective, though as far as he knew no one had ever used a cuss word on the front page of a daily newspaper in Britain before. That in itself would be a scoop of course. First thing back in the office in Fleet Street and he'd try it on the editor. By Christ he would. The 'lads', as they were always called in the *Mirror*, deserved every bit of praise they could get, fighting this capitalistic war for the bosses and their minions.

But it seemed that, at least, some of the minions of the plutocrats cared about the 'lads'. The 'minion' in question came in the guise of a very large, slow and very flat-footed sergeant in the Corps of Military Police; and from the look on his ugly slab-like face he wasn't noticeably impressed by the heroic testimony of the toothless Old Sweat. Indeed he appeared to be decidedly suspicious of it.

As the pressmen dispersed to catch the London train with the rest of the 'heroes of Dunkirk' and the Old Sweat prepared to follow, the sergeant plodded over to where the little man sipped the last of his tea, wishing fervently that it was a 'pint of wallop'. Quietly he remarked, 'Half a mo', laddie. Can I have a look at your AB 64?'

The Old Sweat, who was definitely no 'laddie', did a bit of quick thinking before he replied. For a moment he thought he might do his officer and gent stuff, but then he recalled he was minus his tunic with its major's crowns and the ribbon of the Military Cross. Without that the role wouldn't really work. Hastily he tried another tack: the honest private, who was a little bit afraid of big redcaps. 'Sorry, Sarge, can't help you there.'

'And why's that, laddie?' the policeman asked, humouring the little soldier, who looked like all the barrack-room lawyers he'd ever seen in ten years in the MPs – and he'd seen too many of the crafty buggers.

Swiftly the Old Sweat opened his blanket like some kind of perverted flasher and whined, 'Bin in action, Sarge, lost everything 'cept my pants – and my AB 64 was in my tunic.' He gave the policeman a toothless smile of apology as if he hated to be such a nuisance.

'I see.' The policeman took his time. It was always the best tactic: make the buggers sweat. He sniffed, as if he had just smelled something unpleasant underneath his nostrils. 'Funny though, but you fit the description which we've just received from Froggie land: a major with some kind of frog tart he said was a spy and that's why he had to have a priority to cross the Channel at once. You hear some funny stories these days, don't yer?'

'Spect you do, Sarge. But I never saw no major with a French tart.'

'Course, you didn't, laddie,' the MP sergeant said gently, sliding out his handcuffs with practised ease, 'but we just found a French tart floating in the water near your ferry.' He caught the Old Sweat's arm in a vicelike grip, smiling gently all the while, and put the cuff on him. 'Perhaps you and me might go for a little walk to the castle and have a little talk with my officer? . . . You've bin nicked!'

The recent hero of Dunkirk let his head hang in defeat. He knew he was had.

Two

S he had sobbed as if her heart were broken. She had laughed on the verge of hysteria. Twice she had bent and kissed an embarrassed Major Dalby's hand after he had declared that she was going to be all right and had called her in German '*mein wertes Fräulein . . . und junge Dame*'. In the end, after reassuring Rachel Jacobsohn that they'd look after her father and getting as much of her story out of her as they could under the circumstances, they had asked the duty MO at the castle to give her a shot so that she would sleep for the next twelve hours.

The Old Sweat was a different kettle of fish altogether. He regained his old cocky manner after the first shock of being arrested by the big flat-footed cop and confronted with the corpse of the redhead and the full details of the tale he had told the officer in Dunkirk. 'I just thought I'd do the tart a favour, sir. Seemed a nice French lady,' he lied glibly. 'I was just trying to get her to Blighty and safety. Thought it was my duty to an ally, like.'

'I bet you did,' Dalby said.

The Old Sweat winked at Mackenzie, the fellow 'other rank'. 'Mind yer, sir, if she'd have bin willing to part her legs, like. I wouldn't have said no – natch.' He winked again.

'From what the MO tells me, who examined the body, she'd parted her legs a bit too often, your nice French lady. Now then, Private, let's talk brass tacks. What's this

140

business with the spy you told the officer about over there in Dunkirk?'

The Old Sweat gave in, but only just. 'Well, sir, a bit back before Old Jerry invaded France me and a corporal from our mob went to a knocking shop – excuse me, a house of ill fame—'

Both the Intelligence officers couldn't resist smiling at the fly little old soldier's usage and Dalby said, 'I do know what a knocking shop is, Private.'

'I didn't think officers and gents knew about them sorts of things, sir,' the Old Sweat retorted cheekily.

'Get on with it,' Mackenzie ordered.

'Well, the redhead was the one I took up the dancers for a bit o' the other, but something fishy was going on right from the start—'

'How fishy?' Dalby snapped eagerly, leaning forward to hear every word, for without his false teeth the Old Sweat was hard to follow.

'Well, the tart kept asking questions about our mob and she seemed to know a lot about the old Iron Division—'

'You mean General Montgomery's Third?'

'Yessir. I thought I'd get myself out of there. I could hear men's voices outside as well and they weren't talking Frog either. Sounded like German to yours truly.'

'So what did you do?' Mackenzie asked.

'Well, I had my way with her, like, and then I said we'd go across the road to the little *estaminet* for a wet. She wasn't too keen, but I didn't give her much of chance to refuse. Then I got her and me out of the knocking shop toot sweet. Even went without me best boots, I did.'

'And your corporal?' Mackenzie asked.

The Old Sweat lowered his head, apparently in sudden sadness. Dalby gave Mackenzie a quick look. It signified he knew the Old Sweat was up to his tricks. Mackenzie winked back. He understood, too.

141

The Old Sweat looked up again. 'I don't think I'll ever forgive mesen, sir, for not trying . . .' His voice broke, as if he were trying to stiffle a sob.

'You ought to be on the boards, Private,' Dalby said unfeelingly. 'Get on with it.'

'Well, sir, he'd upped and just disappeared. Never saw the poor young corp agen. And that was about the end of it . . .'

They had sent him back to the Provost Marshal then; he was to remain under close arrest for the time being, but Dalby signed a chitty for urgent dental treatment. The Old Sweat was to be fitted with an upper set as soon as possible, for at the back of his mind Dalby guessed they might need the cunning little reprobate sooner or later and the Old Sweat would be smart enough to maintain that a soldier without teeth couldn't fight. 'No choppers, no grub, no fight' would be his line.

Now the two of them sat, sipping cold cocoa from the cookhouse down below, mulling over what they had just learned and trying to make sense of it. Outside, yet another badly damaged destroyer, listing heavily to port, her structure a mass of twisted wrecked steel, was coming in from Dunkirk, carrying another load of men from the beaches. Both, as they watched, knew that it lent urgency to their discussions. For unless they could stop the unknown 'pianist' he'd go on signalling Wohltorf about the Operation Dynamo sailings and Admiral Ramsey was simply running out of rescue craft.

'So let's look at what we *do* know,' Dalby commenced, emphasizing the words, as if he were a little angry or frustrated. 'One, the Jewish girl has made it clear that there is – *was* – a link between Dunkirk and Dover. Two, this link was – *is* – centred on the – er – knocking shop in Dunkirk. Agreed, Mac?'

'Yessir. And we can take it – three – that the ground

142

link between the two ports is now severed because Fräulein Jacobsohn is now working for us and is no longer in place.'

'Right. So far so good.' Dalby pushed away the mug of cold cocoa and took out his flask. Mackenzie worried about the old man's drinking, but he knew he couldn't tell him to stop it; besides at this moment, he knew too, that Dalby needed it. It was a stimulant that he couldn't do without for long. He waited till the major had poured himself a generous tot and then swallowed it in one gulp. He coughed and his face flushed a hectic red. Then he was ready to go again, eyes sparkling once more with the scotch. 'Four.' Again he ticked off the number on his nicotine-stained fingers. 'Are we any further with this radio location business, Mac? After all, we've got the Navy helping us now.'

'Yes, in a way,' the young sergeant answered hesitantly.

'How d'yer mean – in a way?'

'Well, the RL people have cut down the area of the Jerry pianist's location to that of the general castle area, sir.'

Dalby shot up from his chair. 'You mean from where we are at this very moment, Mac! Then why the bloody hell haven't we done something about it, eh?'

Now it was Mackenzie's turn to flush, not from whisky, but from a kind of embarrassment. 'Well, I mean in the general area of the castle, sir . . . and you mustn't forget the enormous amount of radio traffic coming from here at this very moment. There are hundreds of ships alone in the Channel which are receiving and transmitting signals every hour of the day in connection with Operation Dynamo. It must be the very hell to detect and locate the pianist among all the traffic.'

'Point taken, Mac,' Dalby sat back and relaxed for a few moments. Now there was silence in the little room, broken only by the muted bells of the ambulances racing down the hill from Canterbury, Ashford, and the like, to take off the

wounded that the destroyer was bringing in. For a second
or two Mackenzie forgot the immediate problem and in his
mind's eye tried to picture the chaos and carnage of those
beaches, just twenty odd miles or so away, where the flower
of the British Army was being so cruelly destroyed; where,
if something really drastic was not done, Britain might lose
the war before the week was out.

'Point six,' Dalby resumed the analysis, 'now that the
Jewish girl is in our hands and presumably the link between
Dover and Dunkirk is severed, how will that damned pianist
get his information about our sailings?'

'If I may say so, sir, that's a key point.'

'You may. But you've got more to say, haven't you? You
academic wallahs do like to waffle a lot.'

Mackenzie wasn't offended. He knew the old man was
simply giving him, an other rank, his head: a chance to speak
more fully to a field grade officer, which Dalby was. 'Thank
you, sir. Well I was thinking this. If we could get enough
people together we could surround the whole castle area – it
shouldn't be too difficult, due to the terrain and the limited
access roads. Besides, the castle is well guarded as it is—'

'Go on, Mac,' Dalby said impatiently.

'Anyone who can't provide us with a legimate excuse for
being in the area would then be arrested and questioned.'

'Impossible. We'd need the whole of the Intelligence
Corps to question that number of people. Over a day
there might be hundreds of people who would have to be
interrogated.'

'I understand that, sir. But the Jerry pianist only operates
between certain times. As radio detection has worked out, he
operates on the same frequency and over a time span of thirty
to forty minutes. It's something to do with atmospherics, or
something.'

'Do we know that time span?'

'Yessir,' Mac answered smartly, feeling that Major Dalby

was buying his idea. 'Between twelve and thirteen hundred hours daily. The RT folk say it gives the pianist time to collect information about morning tide sailings from Dunkirk and visuals he can obtain from just looking at Dover harbour over there.'

'That seems to stand to reason,' Dalby conceded. 'And during that period – from twelve to one o'clock, most people are at lunch. There shouldn't be too many folk without sufficient identification wandering about for us to check.'

'And remember this, sir,' Mackenzie added enthusiastically, 'we've got two people now who might be able to speed up any suspicious identification.'

'Fräulein Jacobsohn – and she has good reason to help us now, since she's thrown in her lot with us and we're going to help to try to save . . .' He didn't finish the sentence.

Mackenzie knew why. Dalby wouldn't be able to save her father, the *Herr Doktor*, once her treachery became known to Father Christmas in Berlin. But he didn't raise the matter. As the Germans said, 'You can't make an omelette without breaking eggs.' If the concentration camp inmate had to be sacrificed to help save the British Army in France, well it would have be thus. Hastily he said, 'And that fly little old soldier will cooperate with us, if he knows what's good for him. He's got a charge sheet as long as your arm, sir, I've discovered. Now he can add to that desertion, impersonating an officer and probably nicking the regimental funds, for all I know.'

Dalby allowed himself a wintry smile. It was obvious he was thinking hard again. Suddenly he resumed the discussion with: 'Point seven.'

'Point seven, sir?

'Yes, we've been overlooking the obvious in this whole matter.'

'What's that?'

'The girl – she must have had some means of contacting the pianist?'

'I checked it, sir. She's heard him speak. But she never actually saw him.'

'Well then, how did she give him whatever information she had?'

'She wouldn't tell me, sir,' Mackenzie said somewhat shamefaced.

'Wouldn't tell you!' Dalby exclaimed. 'Why in heaven's name wouldn't she?'

'I thought the same. Why would she protect the Jerry at this late stage of the game when we know about her being blackmailed into spying for the *Abwehr* and all that? Who could be so important to her *here*?'

Dalby looked at the much younger man hard, his face stony, bearing that threatening, no-nonsense look of his which he put on when dealing with obdurate prisoners. 'Well?' he demanded, 'WHO, FOR GOD'S SAKE?'

Feeling a little helpless, even foolish, his face red, Mackenzie stuttered, 'First I checked her identity card, sir. It was an obvious *Abwehr* fake. The writing was almost *Sutterlin**. More importantly the address given for her in Dover doesn't exist.'

Dalby waited impatiently for the answer to his question, but he said nothing.

'Then I reasoned she'd have to have a contact address for the NAAFI. These days, here at Dover, those tea girls are called out at all hours when the boats with the troops arrive. And she had to have that NAAFI contact if she were to carry out her duties for the *Abwehr*. Well, sir she had one and I traced it. To cut a long story short, it was on the London Road. A small rented hall.'

*An old-fashioned form of German handwriting. *Transl.*

Dalby couldn't contain his impatience any longer. 'And?' he snorted.

'It's a makeshift synagogue for Jewish refugees, mostly continental and any of our chaps who are Jewish and want to worship there.' He paused for breath.

Dalby looked at him increduously. 'You mean to say she used someone of her own faith to carry the message to the pianist?'

'That's my theory, sir. Why should she otherwise protect the go-between?'

'God Al-bloody-mighty,' Dalby swore. 'What next? All right, young Mac, what are we bloody well waiting for. Let's go.' With unusual speed for a man of his age he grabbed his webbing pistol belt and started fastening it on.

Outside in the Channel yet another boat started to limp towards the harbour carrying its pathetic cargo of stragglers and beaten soldiers. Time was obviously running out fast . . .

Three

Fog had come in suddenly from the sea. Almost imperceptibly, it had curled itself around Dover like a fat grey cat. Now the streets rising from the front to the heights beyond were damp and dripping, all sound muted and muffled by the wet mist.

Mackenzie, leading the patrol of the West Kent Regiment together with Dalby, told himself it was a scene that could have come straight from Conan Doyle, though he didn't fancy himself in the role of Dr Watson to Dalby's Sherlock Holmes. Still, this venture into the unknown had that nineteenth-century detective story quality about it; all they needed now was the clatter of horse hooves on the damp cobbles and the appearance of a hansome cab.

Mackenzie dismissed the fantasy and cast a glance behind him. The platoon of the West Kents were strung out in single file, fully equipped down to their gas masks slung across their chests, and they carried their rifles at the 'trail', as if they were going into action against an armed enemy. He nodded his approval. Dalby was right in taking this matter very seriously, seriously enough to go straight to Ramsey and ask for this fully armed platoon of the local infantry regiment. After all, with another six destroyers and God knows how many other craft sunk in the Channel between Dunkirk and Dover this day, the most drastic of measures were warranted to stop the devilish handiwork of the unknown pianist.

They turned the bend in the road. Dalby raised his hand and the young subaltern in charge of the platoon, his voice muted, ordered, 'Halt.'

The men stopped, crouched a little, as if they too felt the tension of this fog-bound world which seemed to isolate them from the rest of the human race; it was almost as if they were the last men left alive on earth. Cautiously, while they waited, Dalby went ahead, his hand instinctively falling to the webbing revolver holster at his hip.

Up here the fog was even thicker. He could see the thick white clouds like fluffy cotton wool rolling in from the fields beyond. He narrowed his eyes to get a better view. The makeshift synagogue, he knew from his study of Dover's street plan, was around the other bend. Unfortunately, up here the fog was too thick for him to see it.

Dalby cursed under his breath. The fog was good in one way; it covered their approach. But it was bad too. If the go-between was located in the synagogue, as they suspected now, and he were alerted, it would be easy for him to slip away under the cover of the damned mist.

He wiped the dampness from his face and turned back to the others. 'Lieutenant,' he whispered to the smooth-faced boy in charge of the infantrymen.

'Sir?'

'Send your sergeant with half the platoon to the next fork. Slip round to left and right and you'll come up against the back of the place. Keep in position there and as close up as possible. Stop and arrest anyone who comes out when we go in. And remember,' he added, 'not a sound. Anyone hearing you could do a bunk easily in this fog.'

'Sir.' Hastily the young officer issued his orders and then stole forward to let his sergeant and half the platoon pass on their way to the fork.

Dalby nodded his approval and waited till the men had disappeared into the swirling fog, the sound of their boots so muted by it that they were only audible for a few moments before again there was silence. 'All right, Lieutenant, form your men into a skirmish line. We'll cover the—'

Dalby stopped short. There was the sudden wet hiss of tyres. Somebody was coming down the road at speed on a cycle.

'Look out!' Dalby cried the next moment.

Suddenly, startlingly, a khaki-clad figure appeared out of the mist. It was a soldier, crouched over the handlebars of a government-issue cycle, forage cap tucked down well over his ears against the dampness, going all out downhill.

He saw the men standing there. 'Watch yer backs!' he yelled, not raising his head, and next moment he'd expertly dodged in and out between two of the startled infantrymen and was vanishing down the hill before anyone had the initiative to stop him. But Mackenzie had noted one thing about him. Below the leather jerkin he'd worn, clearly visible on the sleeve of his battledress blouse were the two stripes of a corporal and the black-and-white flash of the Royal Corps of Signals.

'Bloody idiot!' Dalby snorted. 'Nearly had me. Ought to be put on a charge for reckless driving. On government property too.' He dismissed the cyclist. 'Come on, let's get on with it, but all of you keep your weather eye open for more idiots like that.'

Despite the clammy coldness of the fog, the soldiers grinned. Nobody liked corporals. It was good to hear a senior officer rail against them for once.

Now they went in for the final part of their plan. They took up their positions blocking the street. Dalby blew one blast on his whistle. It was echoed by that of the sergeant in charge of the men to the rear of the makeshift camp and church. Dalby said to Mackenzie, 'All right, off we go, Mac.' To the young officer, he added, 'Mark you now, nobody is to get away.'

'Yessir,' the infantry subaltern answered smartly. 'Good hunting, sir.'

'Silly young bugger,' Dalby remarked when they were out of earshot of the piquet line. 'What's he think this is, a bloody fox-hunt?'

Mackenzie grinned to himself. The old man, he told himself, was getting jumpy.

Steadily they advanced up the rest of the steep street. The fog now was so thick that visibility was probably down to five yards. Mackenzie sniffed hard. Often wet fog, he knew, dampened and drained out other odours, but he was distinctively sure he could smell something burning.

'What are you sniffing at like a bloodhound, Mac?' Dalby grunted. 'Don't tell me you've got the bloody "good hunting" kick, too?'

'No sir, but I'm sure I can smell something burning.' He sniffed again. Now he was certain he could.

He opened his mouth to say so, but Dalby cut him off with the exclamation: 'You're right, Mac. Look, there's flames ahead – at one clock!'

Even though the fog was so thick, Mackenzie could see the glow of cherry-red flames leaping up to their right and hear, too, the crackle of wood burning fiercely. 'Come on, sir.' He didn't hesitate now. 'I'm sure it's our place that's on fire!' He started to run, all caution thrown to the wind now.

It was. The flames leaping ever upwards around the rough wooden structure were burning away the fog rapidly so that suddenly everything was coming into sight. The rented hall – it might well have been a one-time church hall, built in the late Victorian period by Methodists, who had been unable to afford much brickwork and had compromised with wood – was burning fiercely, the paint on the wooden front bubbling and blistering like the symptoms of some loathsome skin disease.

'Christ Almighty,' Dalby yelled above the noise, 'the bloody place is burning down. Come on!'

Before Mackenzie could stop him, he had dashed inside, hand held in front of his face against the burning heat, gasping with the shock as it took the very breath out of his lungs. He didn't get far; indeed he almost stumbled and fell, but Mackenzie helped him upright just in time. In the entrance to the place a body lay. It was of a man, whose suit was obviously not of English make and whose body was almost skewered to the floor by the bayonet which had been driven ruthlessly through the small of his back.

'Dead as a doornail,' the MO, who had been hurriedly summoned from the castle, announced rising up from the corpse. 'Somebody gave him a tremendous whack. Strong bugger.' The RAMC captain looked very tired and Mackenzie thought he must have been busy all day with the latest list of casualties off the ships from Dunkirk.

'Thanks, Doctor,' Dalby said. 'Good of you to come with all the work you've got on your hands.'

The MO smiled wearily. 'I can't say it's a pleasure, sir, because it isn't. But it's a long time since I've seen a murder victim, save those that have been done in by Herr Hitler. Do you want me to take care of the stiff for you?'

'Thank you, but no. I'll call for an ambulance when we want him taken care of. You go and get yourself a nice big whisky. You deserve it.'

'And I feel like it.' He shrugged. 'But we're expecting more wounded on the evening tide. So long, sir.'

'So long, Doctor.'

Dalby waited until he was out earshot, walking through the still thick fog to the waiting Humber staff car, then he snapped, 'What have you got, Mac?'

The sergeant looked at his notebook. 'Not much, sir. The dead feller's name is Isaak Rosenblatt. He'd been living in

France, it appears, until quite recently. Came over from Boulogne with other refugees, mostly German and Austrian Jewish, who like him had fled Germany to live in France. He was checked and given a temporary security clearance as long he didn't stay out after an eight o'clock at night curfew and reported to the local bobbies three times a week.'

'A likely candidate then, Mac. German, who lived in France till the balloon went up. Comes over here with a large number of refugees, swamping our immigration people.' Dalby pulled a face. 'Might not even be Jewish. Did you have a look?' he indicated the corpse huddled in a corner, a blanket thrown over him, but with the bayonet still protruding from his back.

'Yessir. He's circumcised all right.'

Dalby sniffed. 'Well, as you know, he won't be the first Jew who worked for the *Abwehr* or the Gestapo, too, for that matter. Anything else?'

'One thing. I checked with a neighbour, a real curtain-twitcher type, proper busybody. Doesn't like Jews much either. Said he'd seen Rosenblatt was often visited by a young woman – "Another one of that lot who killed Our Lord on the Cross", as he put it. Says he thought they were up to no good – "filthy, foreign fornicators" was his phrase.' He allowed himself a faint smile. 'Nice way with words he had, what sir?'

Dalby ignored the comment. 'So we've got a link between Fräulein Jacobsohn and this Rosenblatt recently arrived from France. Anything else?'

Mackenzie hesitated. 'It's just guesswork, sir, but is there a link between the bayonet used to kill the poor swine – a prewar Lee Enfield rifle type—'

'Yes, I know the kind of bayonet. Get on with it.'

'Well, why a bayonet and not, say, an ordinary kitchen knife? Another thing sir, who would know about us and these West Kent chaps? Is the killer a member of the military, someone who might have seen us assembling at Dover Castle and concluded we were coming here, and made his move before we could get to the late Herr Rosenblatt?'

'But that's absurd, Mac, if you'll forgive me,' Dalby snorted.

Mackenzie wasn't offended; he knew Dalby had a short fuse at the best of times. 'Well, sir, wouldn't the average person say it would be absurd to maintain that a Jew, a German Jew in particular, would work for Hitler?'

This time Dalby didn't object to Mackenzie's words. Instead he said slowly, brow furrowed as if he were thinking hard, 'Then there was that bloody fool corporal on his bike who nearly knocked us down – and the man was riding no ordinary bike. It was one of those sit-up-and-beg types that the quartermaster issues to squaddies who are entitled to them for official duties. Christ Almighty –' he snapped his thumb and finger together sharply, eyes suddenly sparkling with renewed energy – 'and the cyclist was in the Royal Corps of Signals!'

Mackenzie saw the way his chief's mind was working immediately. He said, 'If we tie all those items together, sir, and add the fact that the pianist's transmissions are so difficult to locate exactly because they're submerged in all the radio traffic coming from the castle itself, might we conclude that the man who murdered Rosenblatt is perhaps that corporal of Signals on the bike and that the corporal—'

'Is the pianist!' Dalby beat him to the conclusion.

Four

Admiral Ramsey was about at the end of his tether, Dalby could see that. While in the outer offices, telephones jingled, staff officers hurried back and forth, voices were raised as if his staff were excited or angry, perhaps both, he sat slumped at his big desk. There were dark circles under his eyes, his face was very pale and a vein twitched out of control at his right temple. Ramsey would live for another few years before the God of War put his final mark on him, too, but on this June evening with the guns booming out to sea once more, he looked to Dalby as if he might succumb to death at any moment. He waited.

Finally Ramsey spoke. 'Today's losses have been appalling, Major,' he said, his voice lacking all that confident quarterdeck manner of before. 'Hardly dare look at 'em.' With a feeble wave of his big hand he indicated the chart behind him on which were pencilled in the number of men brought home for this day and in the next column what their transportation from Dunkirk to Dover had cost in naval and civilian shipping. 'So I hope you bring me good news. Have you caught this bloody spy yet? I hope you have. We've got to cut down our losses. The Navy will simply bleed white if you don't soon. The other alternative is –' there was a sudden catch in his voice, as if he was afraid to utter the words '– to abandon the operation altogether. And you know, Major, what that would mean . . .' His voice trailed away and Dalby had to strain hard to hear his final words.

Dalby felt sorry for the older man; the strain he was bearing was almost impossible, he knew. So when he spoke, he tried to be enthusiastic about the bold plan which he and Mackenzie had spent half the night trying to work out. It was still crude and risky, but it might just work. 'Sir,' he commenced brightly, 'we haven't got the spy yet, but we know where he is – pretty roughly.'

'Well, why in heaven's name don't you nab him and stop this dreadful leakage of shipping times to the Hun?'

'Because, sir, we want to use him in a much larger scheme to be carried out in the next forty-eight hours, which we think and hope might make the Germans cease their operations against Dunkirk for, say, a couple of days at least.'

'*Cease their operations . . . for a couple of days . . .*' Ramsey stuttered, staring at Dalby, as if he had suddenly gone mad. 'What are you talking about, Major? How can you get that awful Hun feller, Hitler, to stop ops against Dunkirk when his troops are hammering away at our perimeter defence virtually everywhere. Our chaps in the line there must be fighting like tigers to hold the Huns as it is. But . . .' He held his hand to his forehead, as if he felt a sudden pain and could continue no longer.

Dalby waited a moment and continued in an almost conversational manner. 'Perhaps, sir, you recollect the business in 1918 with Colonel Meinertzhagen, who was Allenby's chief-of-intelligence in the desert?'

Ramsey looked up at him, mouth open stupidly. This time, however, he was simply too exhausted to say anything. Dalby saw the look, but continued all the same. 'Well, Meinertzhagen wanted to fool the German–Turkish force about the direction of Allenby's great attack on Turkish-held Jerusalem. To do this he bravely rode into the desert until he encountered a Turkish patrol. As soon as they opened fire on him, he turned his horse and started galloping back to his own lines hell-for-leather. During the chase, he pretended to be hit. He dropped his binoculars, to make it clear that he had originally been spying on the Turkish front, and a specially prepared map case. It contained his name and position so that Johnny Turk wouldn't have much trouble identifying him. It was stained with human blood so that it appeared its owner had been wounded. Above all it contained a doctored map, with Allenby's supposed line of attack marked on it.'

Ramsey shook his head, as if he couldn't understand the world any more. Why was a senior officer of Intelligence telling him this cock-and-bull story about daring-do in the Great War? What had it got to do with his overwhelming problem, for God's sake? Still, he didn't interrupt.

Dalby delivered the end of the tale that had taken place nearly a quarter of a century before. 'Naturally Allenby attacked on a totally different part of the front. He captured Jerusalem and drove the Turks and their German allies out of Palestine. It was an exceedingly successful Intelligence operation which changed the whole future of that part of the Middle East, Admiral.'

Dalby waited in case Ramsey had a question. But he was either too exhausted or bemused to do so. Accordingly the major got down to his reason for the story. 'So, sir, this is what I'm suggesting. We should employ some large-scale imaginative trick, using both this German agent – and others, whose names I won't bother you with – to confuse and blind the Germans to our intentions here and in Dunkirk, an operation which might well give us a few days of grace in which we can get the bulk of the BEF back to the UK.'

'But the Germans know our intention – there is only one thing we can do under the present circumstances,' Ramsey objected somewhat weakly. 'Get our men away as long as we have shipping to do so.' He threw up his hands in an almost Gallic gesture of hopelessness.

'At the moment they do, sir,' Dalby said. 'But it is my intention to both blind them by stopping their sources of

157

information here and in Dunkirk, and at the same time mislead them into thinking we've got a bold plan up our sleeve for France, which would make them hesitate to go the whole hog at Dunkirk.'

Despite his worries and his tiredness Admiral Ramsey showed his interest. 'How do you mean, make them stop, as it were, in Dunkirk?'

'This, sir. I have done some preliminary checking. At present, south of the River Somme, we have the equivalent of two divisions on the L-O-C' – Dalby meant the line-of-communications '– plus the 51st Division retreating in that general direction. Also, there is the 1st Armoured Division, plus a Canadian and the 52nd Lowland disembarking at ports such as Cherbourg etc. We might have as many as six or seven divisions outside the Dunkirk perimeter and, in theory, menacing the German left flank.'

Now Ramsey started to show interest. 'Go on,' he urged.

'Well, sir, what if we could convince the Germans that this force was being built up from ports from Dover down to Newhaven and that it appeared we intended to attack the over-extended German flank—'

'Why, the Hun might re-group and prepare for that attack,' Ramsey cut in. 'They'd certainly keep their armoured divisions, now ready to make the final thrust at Dunkirk, back to prepare a counter-stroke.' The sudden enthusiasm vanished from his pale face as abruptly as it had appeared. 'But how could we convince them that we were reinforcing the British forces south of the River Somme? Their spies, both here and in Dunkirk would tell them otherwise, wouldn't they?'

Dalby smiled and it was not a very pleasant smile. 'Sir, those spies,' he said very deliberately, 'will keep their eyes closed and obey my orders or their eyes will be shut – *permanently*. Now, with your permission, I'm going to tell you, Admiral, what I and my sergeant are intending doing . . .'

All that day Dalby and Mackenzie worked out the details of their plan, knowing that it was a race against time. Fortunately they were in possession of a note written by Admiral Ramsey himself in his own hand, ordering every-one, regardless of rank, to 'cooperate fully with Major Dalby and his team or face the consequences'. The note opened all doors, even those of the stuffiest, hide-bound senior staff officer.

They had decided that Dalby, as the older of the two and the least fit, should take over the business of locating and arresting the pianist, who had been on the air again briefly that very morning. He would be assisted, though she didn't know it yet, by the girl. Once they had told her of the brutal murder of Herr Rosenblatt, they were certain she would cooperate fully in the apprehension of the pianist.

Naturally she had never met the radio operator, but she *had* heard his voice when she had been still hidden in the chain locker. They hoped that when they contacted a suspect – and they were going to call all the signals corporals in the garrison by phone – she might be able to identify their man by his voice.

As Mackenzie had pointed out previously, 'We are fairly sure he's located here in the castle. And there can't be too many corporals in the Royal Signals in the place. We'll go through the lot of them on some pretext or other with her listening. By then, what with the murder and everything, I think, sir, Fräulein Jacobsohn will be as keen as mustard to assist us. Besides,' he had added a little hesitantly, glancing covertly at Dalby, 'she does think we're going to so something about her father in the concentration camp.'

Dalby had grunted, but had made no further comment, though Mackenzie could guess that he was thinking that Herr Jacobsohn wouldn't have much of a future if things went wrong now.

'Your task will be easier in a way over there,' Dalby had

pointed out. 'With that old lead-swinger' – he meant the Old Sweat – 'showing you the way to his damned knocking shop and pointing the finger at this Madame Giselle and her ladies of Dunkirk, that part won't be difficult.' He had frowned and sucked his teeth as if he had suddenly discovered a bad one there.

'But getting her and the others back to Dover might well be. From what I hear this morning, the situation in Dunkirk is getting progressively more dicey.' He looked hard at the younger man.

Mackenzie felt like smiling, but he didn't. He told himself that these days the old man was becoming a real old mother hen, fussing over him all the time. 'Not to worry, sir,' he reassured Dalby, 'I'll pull it off, as the actress said to the bishop.'

Dalby wasn't amused at the witticism.

Hastily Mackenzie added, 'Besides I'm taking that platoon of hairy-arsed West Kents with me. I've got their CO's permission to do so. According to their subaltern, they're "burning with desire to get to grips with the Hun". Cold steel and all that, what.' He chuckled. 'A real fire-eater, that officer is, sir.'

'And he might well be a dead fire-eater, if he doesn't watch his step,' Dalby commented sourly.

Mackenzie didn't respond. Suddenly his mind was full of the awesome responsibility of the task ahead. If he and the major didn't pull it off, just two ordinary soldiers tackling – indirectly – the armed might of the Third Reich, not only might Britain fall, but also, step by step, the British Empire as well. It was not a pleasant thought for a young man, all of twenty-four years of age . . .

PART FIVE:
THE MAKING OF A PIANIST

One

'You've no right to do this to me, sir,' the Old Sweat whined. Slowly the naval launch which had brought them across the Channel was approaching the crowded beaches. Everywhere there was smoke rising mingled with the blood-red flashes of exploding artillery shells. Wreckage was everywhere. Sunken craft on all sides, and beyond, close to the beaches themselves, there were the blackened grotesque shapes of burned-out vehicles and the wreckage of shattered houses. All were silhouetted against the angry red glare of the sky over the agony of dying Dunkirk.

'Just got back from the frigging place and now back I am here in frigging Dunkirk. Got my rights yer know, Major, even though I am only a common squaddie.' The Old Sweat's wrinkled face contorted into a look of self-pity. 'An' I ain't got no choppers to eat with. That's agen King's Regulations, Major.'

The newly created 'Major' Mackenzie looked down at the Old Sweat – naturally, being the Old Sweat, he was sheltering behind the gunwale of the little craft, as tracer zipped back and forth across the water in white lethal fury.

'Oh, do put a sock in it, will you,' he said calmly, as if he were used to commanding a squad of infantrymen in tight situations like they found themselves at this moment. After all, the whole of the British Army in France was only too eager to kiss goodbye to '*la belle France*'. They were actually going back into the place. 'Do your job. Show us this knocking shop of yours and the sooner you get us there, the sooner you'll be going back to Blighty. Now shut up, I'm concentrating.'

Mackenzie was indeed.

He could guess that while the regular infantry regiments still on the beaches would be orderly and disciplined, the second-line troops and those of the supply services, without any battle-experienced officers to command, might well be more of a bloody nuisance than the Germans themselves. In particular he would have to ensure that the young midshipman, who looked barely sixteen, kept well out of the way of the troops. They might well storm his motorboat and that would be that. All the documents he had with him signed personally by Admiral Ramsey would cut no ice with a mob of squaddies desperate to get back to Dover before the Germans arrived in force.

Mackenzie hesitated no longer. Time was now of the essence. Hurriedly he told the midshipman in charge what he was to do, informed him that he and his skeleton crew were to open fire on any unauthorized troops trying to board his craft, gave him the details of the signals he would use from the beach once he had hopefully returned there with his prisoners, and then leaving the pale-faced boy, with his ears sticking out from beneath the over-large steel helmet looking very worried, he and the West Kents splashed over the side into the waist-deep water filled with floating corpses and debris, and began to wade to the beach.

It seemed to take them an age to reach the beach. Time and time again they were forced to duck as long-range German shells slammed into the water, showering them with a fury of whirling white water, shrapnel hissing lethally to all sides. Then they were sinking and plodding their way through ankle-deep loose sand until they reached the gaunt skeletons of the houses which had once made up the place's promenade.

'My God, sir,' the keen young West Kents' subaltern said in an awed voice, 'it's like a hell's kitchen.'

'That it is,' Mackenzie was forced to agree, shouting above the tremendous racket. For to their immediate front there was one long continuous line of blazing buildings, shaking under each new impact like stage decorations, a high wall of fire roaring like a furnace, vicious purple tongues of flame reaching out for the infantrymen as if intent on sucking them into this maelstrom of fire.

Strung out in a cautious file, each infantryman carrying his weapon at the high port ready to go into action immediately, they made their way along the mole, with giant flames leaping a hundred feet or more to left and right into the sky, the heat sucking the very air out of their lungs so that at times they were gasping and choking for breath like ancient asthmatics in the throes of a fatal attack. Still, the youthful West Kents plodded on, ignoring the comments of the battered veterans of the perimeter infantry, heading now in groups of fifty under their officers and NCOs for the beaches: 'Yer going the wrong way, chums . . . Gonna get yer knees brown, sonny . . .' But the West Kents ignored the comments, most of them ribald, loyally following their keen young second-lieutenant into this crazy world of fire and flame and dead hand destruction.

Mackenzie felt proud of them. He told himself that as long as Old England produced youngsters like these boys in their smart khaki uniforms and polished boots, as if they were still on the parade ground of their depot, the country would survive. The Old Sweat was not so sure. Every step into the dying port seemed to take him an effort of will to make. Time and time again, he whined in a litany of self-pity and some fear, 'I ought not to be here by rights . . . It's not ruddy fair.'

Finally Mackenzie, losing patience with the old soldier, snapped, 'Nothing's bloody fair, get that through yer bloody thick skull. Now stop moaning . . . or I'll have you on a fizzer tootsweet.'

Mackenzie's tone must have frightened him somewhat, for now the Old Sweat started to give him the directions they needed. Obviously he had finally come to the conclusion that the sooner they found the knocking shop and did what they had come here to to do, the sooner he, personally, would be back on that launch heading for Dover.

But it seemed to Mackenzie as they penetrated ever deeper into the burning chaos of the port area that there were British soldiers there who were too drunk, or 'bomb-happy' as they called it, to care whether they stayed here or went back to their own country. Some indeed appeared mad or to be playing at being mad.

In the cellars and basements of their wrecked or burning buildings, British soldiers were skulking everywhere, drinking, ranting, shouting. Once they came across an emaciated soldier virtually naked, save for a towel wrapped around skinny loins, proclaiming himself to be Mahatma Gandhi and invoking Hindu gods to save them if they would give up armed resistance. The West Kents subaltern, red with anger, .38 revolver in his hand, asked Mackenzie's permission to shoot him there and then. Mackenzie refused. He guessed anything drastic now might well provoke serious trouble among these drunken deserters, who seemed to have forgotten that they were British soldiers.

Others were reeling from side to side, either drunk or hysterical, ignoring the bombs and shells, weeping like broken-hearted children, hugging dolls or looted teddy bears to their chests, as if the toys were their last comfort before death overtook them.

'Christ All-bleeding-Mighty', the Old Sweat proclaimed, 'fancy being brought back to this. They've all got the bloody Doolalli Tap!'

Mackenzie didn't know what the 'Doolalli Tap' was, but

he could guess. He shouted so that all of them could hear. 'As long as we stick together, lads, and follow orders, none of us is going to go barmy – and remember this: me and your officer are going to get you out of this mess, come what may. Now, let's just keep moving and ignore them!'

He indicated a crazy man, who was carrying an ornate cross looted from some local church, running back and forth wildly and screaming like some lost soul, 'The Lord have mercy on us. Christ have mercy on us. Down on your knees, you sinners, and pray to the Lord God for mercy . . . Do you hear? PRAY!'

Despite everything, however, they started to make progress and Mackenzie was glad to clear the immediate port and beach area and its crazy cowards. Now the crowds of deserters and stragglers had begun to thin out. Here and there they even found small parties of infantrymen dug in, looking weary, unshaven and hungry, but determined. These men were still commanded by their officers and NCOs and Mackenzie didn't need to be told that these were last-ditch defenders of Dunkirk. Once the outer perimeter gave way, which would be soon if Dalby's plan didn't work, these would be the ones who were to fight to the last to allow the last survivors to escape, that is if the German armour didn't overtake them before they could reach the beach and the waiting ships.

'Not far now, Major,' the Old Sweat proclaimed. 'I recognize that *estaminet* on the corner there. Once went in for a beer. Real frog gnat's piss it was—'

'All right,' Mackenzie cut him off sharply, 'spare us your memoirs. Save 'em for the great reading public. Mr Gollancz'd love 'em.'

'Mr Gollancz? Never heard of him, sir,' the Old Sweat said, puzzled.

Mackenzie didn't attempt to enlighten him, for abruptly he was assailed by an eerie, almost electric feeling that

167

something had gone wrong; that trouble loomed ahead: bad trouble.

Indeed in that very same instant, there was a sharp crack like a twig breaking underfoot in a summer-dry wood. *Thwack*! A slug slammed into the wall next to him only feet away. He recoiled, as if stung. A rifle spat fire again. Just behind him one of the West Kents yelped in sudden agony. His hand shot to his shoulder.

'Bugger this!' he cursed, as bright red blood arced out of the wound, seeping through his fingers. He staggered and nearly fell. A moment later the young officer caught him, yelling at the same time, 'Hold fast. Prepare to return fire!'

Under other circumstances, Mackenzie would have laughed. The commands sounded like something out of a nineteenth-century imperial drama, fighting the 'pesky Pathan' and all that. But not now. He didn't want to get involved in some protracted fire-fight now. Time was running away. 'Ready to move off,' he countermanded the young subaltern's order, as a burly man in the uniform of the Coldstream Guards stepped out of the doorway to his right, two inverted stripes on the sleeve of his once immaculate uniform indicating that he had served six years in the army.

Mackenzie flashed an angry glance in the guardsman's direction and cried, 'Did you fire that fucking shot? . . . What the hell do you think you're at?'

The big soldier took it all very calmly. 'I could have killed him if I'd wished,' he answered coolly. 'I was a marksman back at Purbright.'

A furious Mackenzie ignored the comment. 'Don't give me all that bullshit,' he cried. 'I asked you a question. Now bloody well get out of my way, if you know what's good for you.'

The guardsman reacted totally differently from what Mackenzie expected. He thrust his two fingers into his mouth and whistled shrilly. Suddenly khaki-clad figures started to appear at windows and from doorways on both sides of the narrow cobbled street. With them came screaming drunken whores, some of them half naked with the soldiers fondling their bottoms and breasts and, in one case, actually thrusting himself back and forth against the bare rump of one of the women, groaning mightily as he did so.

'I say, sir,' the young subaltern gasped, 'what the devil's going on?'

But it was the Old Sweat, not Mackenzie, who answered the question for him. 'It's the knocking shop area, sir. We've found it!'

As angry as he was, Mackenzie couldn't help but give a sigh of relief. Now they could find this Madame Giselle woman and get on their way back to the naval launch before the balloon went up here in Dunkirk. But he was mistaken. It wasn't going to be as easy as all that.

Just as he was about to give the order to advance, the guardsman held up his big hand like a cop controlling traffic and growled, 'You're not going any further, Major. This is Free England now.' Behind him the more sober of the deserters raised their weapons menacingly and the soldier with his pants around his ankles made a clumsy attempt to pull them up, while at the same time pounding at the whore, who was wriggling her naked white rump for all she was worth.

'What do you mean?' Mackenzie snapped, his anger growing by the moment at this mob and in particular at its leader. 'What the hell do you—'

'I'll tell you, Major,' the guardsman cut him off. 'Your kind is finished. All that officer and gent bullshit. Your lot landed us in this frigging mess and then buggered off and left us to look after oursens. Well that's what we're doing. We're looking after oursens and gonna have a good time before the Jerries put us in the bag. We've got tarts, we've got all the

169

grub we want in the quartermaster's stores and we've got enough booze to sink a frigging battleship. So we're not having your kind coming back here, ordering us around.' His eyes narrowed and suddenly Mackenzie realized he was facing no blowhard, full of drink-induced piss and vinegar. The guardsman wouldn't hesitate; he'd kill in cold blood, if he had to. Slowly his own hand slipped down to his pistol holster. There was no going back now. This was the showdown.

Two

'*Schweinerei!*' the Signal Corps corporal cursed as he eyed himself in the metal shaving mirror nailed to the wall of his little billet in the castle. '*Bisher alles OK, aber verdammte Scheisse!*' In the manner of lonely or secretive men he often talked to himself when he was alone, which was now, but rarely did he let his guard down to do so in German, his native language.

But this was a special situation. For days now he had felt a sense that they were closing in on him. His long training in the Reich and then in Belgium had made him constantly on his guard, aware of new and potentially dangerous developments, even before they happened. Here in the castle, he was right in the centre of things and although naval and other of the British intelligence services kept a low profile, he had sensed for at least three days now – ever since the murder of the Yid – that the hated English counter-spies had been working flat out. He had even pinpointed a couple of the more dangerous of them – an aged major who wore the ribbons of the Old War – God Almighty he might have been one of the swines who had murdered his father back in 1916 – and the young staff sergeant with his handsome mug, but cunning, far too clever, dark eyes.

He looked at his own handsome image in the little steel mirror again and said, this time in English, 'Don't worry, Papa, the bastard English won't murder me in cold blood like they did you in Dublin.' He sniffed – for all his acquired ruthlessness and inherited hatreds, he was still often overcome by that unique Irish sentimentality that no other race on earth seemed to possess. As old Father Christmas had once remarked thoughtfully to him back in Berlin, gently stroking one of his fat little dachshunds, 'You're a funny race, the Irish, hard as nails in some cases, more damned sentimental than the Germans in others. But never mind, my dear Kurt, or should I call you Tim again, that sentimentality is good for an agent. It makes him sensitive to atmosphere and other people's motives.'

For a few moments he stood there impassively, thinking of what Father Christmas had said, and then moving back to his dead father and Irish patriots, who he knew only from faded yellowing photographs, taken thirty or forty years before, and his dear sick mother's stories . . .

The English had murdered his father back in Dublin that Easter. They had dragged him out of the post office, badly wounded as he had been, bleeding like a stuck pig, and had propped him up on a hard chair the soldiers had found somewhere in the smoking wreckage of the area. He had begged for water – all the patriots taken prisoner by the English had – but he hadn't gotten any.

Instead they had given him a mock trial: a couple of their tough front-line officers in their battered caps and soiled trenchcoats, with revolvers and hand grenades hanging from their belts, had asked, 'How do you plead, rebel?'

According to those of the 'boys' who had got away in the confusion of the final surrender, his father had said boldly, 'Not guilty. I fight for a Free Ireland.'

The officers had taken it in their stride. They had not even laughed at this middle-aged intellectual with his gold-rimmed glasses and pale academic face pretending to be a soldier fighting for the cause of Irish freedom. They had called the clerk of the court, and recorded a verdict of guilty

172

– death by firing squad. Bring in the next of the treacherous bastards!

According to the boys who had come to Germany after the war and told his poor grieving mother the whole sad story, the English swine had sat him on his chair against a bullet-pocked wall and shot his dad out of hand without so much as a priest to give him the last rites, and then one of those swaggering loutish front-line bastard officers had turned over the body contemptuously with the toe of his boot and found his father was still breathing. Without hesitating or taking his pipe from between his lips, he had pressed his big .38 to the back of his father's head and blown his skull away. That done, he'd swaggered off drinking whisky from a pocket flask like a workman who was having his tea break.

Looking at his face in the mirror, Tim Kerrigan remembered the scene as vividly as if he had been there personally, though he'd been a mere baby when it had all happened. But then he had heard the story over and over again from his mother.

Naturally his mother, who was German, had told him the tale in her own language, but later when he had grown up somewhat, some of the boys who could afford it had come to post-war Berlin and had told him the tale in English, apeing the la-di-da English of the officers who had shot his father and the cries and pleas in the soft brogue of the south, so that the story of his father's death in the battle for Ireland's freedom had seemed even more poignant and realistic and had made him hate the English swine even more.

By the time war had come in August 1939, when Germany had marched into Poland, and he had volunteered as an Irishman without an Irish passport for the *Wehrmacht*, it was obvious which way his military career was going to go. Indeed, he had secretly wished, as he underwent the

173

brutal training of the average *Wehrmacht* recruit, that his future military assignment would be in military intelligence: working against the English in the country of his father's birth – Ireland.

It hadn't altogether worked out, but within two months of leaving the Potsdam infantry depot with a recommendation that he should be commissioned into the elite 9th Berlin Infantry Regiment, although he wasn't German, he had been assigned instead to the *Abwehr*. As Father Christmas had told him at his initial interview, 'After all, *Fahnrich** Kerrigan, what better candidate for active service with the *Abwehr* could we have than you? The son of a pro-German Irish patriot who died for his country in the field. A fluent speaker of English and your country's native Gaelic –' the little white-haired admiral had looked embarrassed for some reason at the mention of Gaelic – 'plus your undoubted intelligence and military ability, even though it's only with the poor old stubble-hoppers.' Father Christmas had meant the infantry. 'No, you're our man, *Herr Fahnrich*. Well, what do you say, young man?'

He hadn't hesitated for an instant. He had jumped at the chance to work directly for Ireland, though it hadn't turned out to be quite what he had expected. He had thought, after training, he would be sent straight to Northern Ireland to work with the IRA and commence the new revolution there. He had been in for a disappointment.

A month later he had completed his *Abwehr* agent's training, including radio transmission work and, commissioned a second lieutenant, he had been summoned to Berlin to meet Father Christmas once again to be told: 'You are in due course to be sent to a special group we are assembling in England as a pianist.'

'A pianist, sir?' he had echoed.

---

*Officer-Cadet. *Transl.*

'A radio operator.'

'But I thought, sir, I'd be on active service in Ireland.' He had attempted to object.

The little white-haired head of the *Abwehr* wouldn't have it. 'No, *England*,' he had answered firmly, 'and you'll be on active service all right. Remember, if the Tommies catch you, it'll mean your head. They'll string you, after a trial. The English are a cruel people, as you know from your own father's fate.' The Admiral knew his Irish well, as he did the English. Off and on he had been working with the Irish and against the English since 1916. The former were often unreliable, especially when they were in their cups. With the Irish, the English didn't need to be particularly cruel; the Irish mostly did their work for them.

He had looked hard at the handsome young lieutenant with his wide-open honest face, as if he were seeing his face for the very first time; almost as if, too, he were trying to detect those fatal Irish weaknesses, which would inevitably lead him to the gallows like his father before him: a weak intellectual talker, who should never have risked going back to Ireland with Roger Casement in the first place. But seemingly he could find none. So he'd gone on to explain, 'First, however, you will be sent to neutral Belgium. There we have a group of Flemish nationalists who are working together with certain of our people. You will gain practical experience there before you are sent to England.' The Admiral had given him that careful smile of his, saying, 'Don't look so disappointed, young friend. Your day will come sooner than you think. Then I am confident you will do great things that will, in the final analysis, help the cause of your father's country.'

At the time he hadn't noticed that Father Christmas' reference had been to his 'father's country' and not to his own. If he had, he might have guessed that for the *Abwehr* chief, his country was Germany and it was for the Reich he

175

was working and not for some romantic notion of an Ireland that he had never even visited.

He hadn't liked West Flanders. It was dull and flat and the Flemings he had worked with had seemed the same. They were peasants really: distrustful, greedy, without wit or a sparkle of charm. Even the brothels he was allowed to visit once a week on Friday night (under armed supervision) were the same. The whores were without passion or imagination. He paid his money. They opened their legs. They grunted a couple of times routinely when he entered them and then presumably looked at the ceiling while he had sexual intercourse, as if on his own. Every time afterwards, he told himself it was 'hardly worth the bloody effort'.

In the spring of 1940, he actually jumped at the chance to go on a mission which they informed him right at the beginning might well be a 'one-way one'. Apparently he was to drop into England to take up his task as a pianist, and they said his predecessor had been caught within days and had been shot in the Tower of London 'in null comma, nix seconds'. For the English were 'hard cruel bastards'.

The information had not worried him. 'Bad cess on 'em!' he had retorted hotly. 'The English'll have to get up earlier if they're gonna catch Tim Kerrigan's son.'

And he had been right – at first. The *Abwehr* had given him a perfect cover, well he'd thought so in the beginning. He was to be a signals corporal in the British 3rd Infantry Division, Signals. The AB 64 and the other military documents were perfect, taken from some dead Tommy. They'd even changed the dead man's place of birth to Dublin to account for his Irish accent when he spoke English, making out he'd volunteered from neutral Eire to fight fascism and the hated Germans.

But the crowning achievement of the *Abwehr* was to have him 'transferred' from France, where the Third was located at that time, to Dover Castle itself, right in the middle of the great signals network where his high-speed morse transmissions, none of them lasting more than a minute or two, would be exceedingly hard to locate, even if the enemy detector vans knew he was operating from that area. There were just too many signals coming and going from the castle. Whoever had thought of the daring plan, he had told himself, to place an *Abwehr* pianist right in the midst of the enemy headquarters, deserved the Iron Cross First Class!

He had no trouble with his fellow squaddies. They took to him from the start. They realized soon that, although he was a Paddy, a Mick from the bogs, he was very intelligent and knew his business. That surprised him. With his background, he'd expected them to be stand-offish and very English, like those middle-class Englishmen his mother had known before the Great War. They weren't. Naturally, they made jokes about the 'Ould Sod' and 'Mick brickies'. But they stood him half pints in the wet canteen off duty and took him to the flicks when their girlfriends had a spare tart who needed a 'cuddle in the one and a tanners'. Indeed, at times he had to remind himself these were the descendants of the men who had killed his father so long before. In fact, he liked them better than the stiff-necked SS men he had trained with and their bloody silly racial theories and heel-clicking self-importance, which had bored him out of his mind at times.

Indeed, it had been one of his fellow English corporals who had warned him inadvertently two days before that there was danger on the horizon. They had both ended a long day of coding and transmitting by going into the town to ease the strain with an egg and chip supper, 'and don't go easy on the tomato ketchup, ma!' Afterwards, while they'd been savouring a cup of 'real tea' with plenty of sugar, Bill, the other corporal, had remarked casually, 'Did yer know there's a flap going on, Mick?'

He had long given up telling his fellow corporals that his

first name was Tim. To them, as an Irishman, he was either Mick or Paddy. So he didn't try to correct Bill. Instead, he had said in a bored fashion, 'No, what is it? We've knocked the spots off old Jerry in France?'

'Come off it, mate. Ring the other one, it's got bells on it. Ner, it's this. This shift, so I've been told by me muckers, they've been ringing signals corporals and asking 'em a load of daft questions. Yer know, where did yer train – Catterick or Colchester? . . . How many years o' service have yer got? Just a load of time-wasting old bull, as if they just wanted to keep our blokes – all up to their necks in work – talking.' He took another drag at his Woodbine. 'Can't figure it out mesen. But then you know them officers and gents. They're all "bullshit baffles brains".'

'Yer, yer probably right,' he had answered apparently casually and had changed the subject. But already at the back of his mind the alarm bells had begun to ring urgently. There was something going on, he knew it in his bones – and whatever it was, it was concerned with him.

For the first time since he had started this mission as pianist operating right in the middle of the enemy camp, Tim Kerrigan-Schulze, the son of one of Ireland's heroes of the Great Battle of the Dublin Post Office in 1916, felt afraid. Suddenly, it came to him, an almost choking feeling at the knowledge of what would happen to him if the English caught him now, as they seemed to be trying to. Pierrepoint, the official hangman, would tie that rope knot to the right of his Adam's apple, while his assistant slipped the black hood over his head. There'd be a moment of absolute terror and blindfolded confused horror. A sudden sharp crack and he'd be falling into eternity, his neck snapping at the moment of extinction.

Now in the tight confines of his little room, his lean body suddenly wet with a hot sweat, he stared at his contorted face in the mirror, realizing that this was how his father must have felt before they had shot him to death. Was he going to go the same way, cursed to die young, his life cut off before he had really begun to live it, fated to be buried in some dark unhallowed ground without even being a hero: just a treacherous spy?

'*Was soll ich machen?*' he croaked at himself in the mirror. '*Was kann ich machen . . . Bitte?*'*

But his mirror image remained obstinately silent. Like all traitors and spies in the end, the pianist was on his own, with every man's hand against him.

---

*What shall I do? What can I do . . . Please?'. *Transl.*

Three

'There's a brothel up there,' Mackenzie said very slowly and very clearly. The Germans had ceased firing into Dunkirk for a while and his words echoed and re-echoed down the stone chasm of the ruined street. 'I'm going to fetch the owner from it . . .' He paused and looked at the big guardsman. 'Whether you like it or not.'

'Leave the tarts alone,' the guardsman replied coldly, 'if you know what's best for you.'

'Yer,' the drunken mob echoed, their brutalized unshaven faces revealing that they were out of control and they were capable of anything. Mackenzie realized this as here and there he heard them clicking off the safety catches of their weapons.

The guardsman's defiance allied to that sound made him burn inside with sudden fury. He had never expected British soldiers to descend to these depths and he was not going to tolerate it, come what may. Next to him, the Old Sweat hissed urgently, 'Better try some other way, sir. This little lot is out for trouble, real trouble. Stop at nothing.'

Mackenzie ignored him. Instead, he flushed angrily and, staring up at the guardsman, snapped, 'Get out of my way.'

Behind him the subaltern gasped. He, too, was realizing that the British soldier could be just as bolshy as the French rabble they had encountered earlier on.

Again Mackenzie took no notice. He realized he was

dealing with a mob and the thought flashed through his mind that this was going to be the way it would be in the future. There'd be other mobs – lots of them – like this. If the British, normally so tame and obedient, had gone bolshy, then the only way to deal with them was to be even more bolshy than they were. Abruptly he knew exactly what he had to do. 'I shall not tell you again, Guardsman, but you move that rabble out of my way and let me get on with my job, or it will be the worse for *you*, personally.'

The guardsman looked at him contemptuously. 'You and whose army, mate?' he asked.

Mackenzie's anger grew. Now he made a show of unbuttoning the flap of his pistol holster and drawing out his .38. He spoke softly so that the mob had to strain to hear what he said. 'Move these men out of my way. I'll give you up to three.'

The guardsman wasn't impressed. He sneered, 'You can give me up to a hundred and fucking three if you—'

Mackenzie had had enough. Without appearing to aim, he pulled the trigger. The big pistol jerked upwards. The guardsman howled with pain, high-pitched and hysterical like a woman in agony. His rifle clattered to the pavement. 'You rotten mean bastard,' he began. Then his shattered right knee gave away and he dropped, either unconscious or dead with shock even before he hit the ground.

Mackenzie wasted no further time. 'Lieutenant,' he cried above the sudden racket from the mob, 'turn your Bren on anyone who attempts to get in our way.'

'Yessir,' the young officer, his eyes gleaming with admiration, sang out at once. 'Will do.'

But there was no need for any further action. The drunken mob was already moving, muttering sullenly, but moving back all the same. The spirit of defiance had gone out of them and Mackenzie knew he'd won. It was going to be a lesson for the future: hit the ringleader and the

181

mob would give in immediately. Basically they were all cowards.

Five minutes later they were on their way up the street for their final rendezvous with Madame Giselle and her Dunkirk knocking shop. By now it was completely dark save for where the fires still raged. The sudden silence after the artillery bombardment and the disappearance of the cowed mob, leaving their dead leader to stiffen on the bloody cobbles in the evening cold, gave the street an eerie feeling. It was, thought Mackenzie, as if behind the shuttered windows and doors of the still intact houses there were anxious people hidden from view, ears pressed against the openings, trying to pick up any suspicious sound. Mackenzie didn't know exactly what might happen, but he was sure that it might well be something lethal. For in this dying Dunkirk, everything and anything could happen.

He had taken the lead again, accompanied by a very reluctant Old Sweat. But there was no other choice for the aged regular. He was the man who was going to identify the knocking shop owner. Not that the Old Sweat thought it would do any good even if they did apprehend her. 'You'll never get that old cowbag to work with us,' he stated categorically. 'She's a bloody real hard case. Give her a tash and she could be a ringer for our old sarnt-major before the war.'

'Let that be my worry,' Mackenzie attempted to soothe the little man.

'Yer, I don't want it. That big Flemish bint is as tough as nails. Believe you me, sir. Maybe,' he shrugged, 'yer might be able to get her to talk if yer bribed her. But I don't even think that would work. Anyway, sir, how we gonna get into her frigging knocking shop before she does a bunk or her and her mates start popping off at us?'

He suddenly stopped.

'You mean we're here?'

182

'Too true, sir. That's the place over there. I remember it well.' He rubbed his genitals, as if he were illustrating just *how well* he remembered the Dunkirk knocking shop.

For a moment or two, Mackenzie stared at the undamaged brothel, though its windows were cracked and shattered into spider webs which glistened in the reflected flames of the fires further up the cobbled street. There was no one in sight, but yet again Mackenzie was overcome by the feeling that there were eyes and ears behind those cracked windows, watching and listening tensely.

'Gonna be a tough nut to get into,' he mused almost as if speaking to himself. 'If we tackle the front, and the doors are barred, the chickens might well have time to flee the coop.' He frowned.

'Yer,' the Old Sweat agreed, 'and I wouldn't put it past her nibs to put up a real fight for the place.'

'Why go through the front?' the young West Kents officer suggested.

'But the back way could be just as bad. They could defend that too, you know,' Mackenzie objected.

'I'm not suggesting that either, sir,' the West Kent said smartly. 'I'm talking about mouse-holing, sir.'

'*Mouse-holing*?' Mackenzie exclaimed, but already the young subaltern was issuing his orders sotto voce . . .

Five minutes later they were grouped around a house further up the street, perhaps three doors away from the brothel, hidden in the dark shadows, with two of the infantrymen making a rough-and-ready platform with their crossed rifles. Without a command, a third now heaved himself on to the platform and, balancing awkwardly on it, allowed himself to be raised. Reaching upwards to the nearest upstairs window sill, he pulled himself on to it and, regaining his wind, dropped his rifle sling to those waiting below before tackling the roof gutter. Next minute he was on the roof itself, noiselessly tackling the ancient slates with his bayonet, cutting the nails and making a gap big enough for a man to ease himself through the lathes below.

Mackenzie nodded his head approvingly. Now he knew what mouse-holing meant. 'Good show,' he whispered. 'Carry on chaps.'

As always, the Old Sweat wasn't impressed. In a surly manner he said under his breath to himself, 'Good show! Bloody types like that could get yer killed toot-bloody-sweet!'

Within five minutes and almost noiselessly, the infantry-men, using hands and their bayonets, had worked their way from the slate roof of the first old house into the loft of the second one, the same loft that the ill-fated young corporal of Signals had used to make his escape under the guidance of the Jewish girl. Now, the leading West Kents had pulled their spare grey socks over their boots so that they made no noise as they worked their way through the darkness of the upper storeys which stank of bird droppings and old age.

Mackenzie and the Old Sweat followed, revolvers in their hands, ready for instant action; for faintly now they could hear muted voices coming from the next house which was the Dunkirk knocking shop where all the trouble had first started. Mackenzie guessed that the voices belonged to the whores and the Belgian men who were their protectors. He prayed they'd keep on talking. Once they stopped, it would mean that they had been rumbled, and in the confines of the loft they would be bound to suffer casualties; and taking a hard line on the matter, Mackenzie knew, too, that casualties would slow them up on their return to the waiting launch. Then he'd be forced into yet another decision he hated (as he had been with the cocky drunken guardsman): should he simply abandon his wounded to their fate? After all, the fate of the remaining troops in France depended upon his returning the women back to Dover as speedily as possible.

But now another sound commenced, impinging itself on his mind, which made him forget his other problems. It was that of hectic breathing, as if someone was hyperventilating; indeed for a crazy moment he thought it could be that of someone at the height of sexual ectasy. He dismissed the thought the next moment and concentrated on the task at hand, as before him the two leading mouse-holers prepared to break through the final barrier into the knocking shop itself.

They hesitated. They looked at Mackenzie in the gloom. He nodded. Behind him the rest of the West Kents raised their rifles, ready for instant action. Mackenzie felt his right hand holding the .38 suddenly grow wet with sweat. It was his nerves, he knew. Abruptly he said a quick prayer, asking that they would break through and get the drop on the enemy inside before they could react. All hell would be let loose if wild shooting commenced in this confined space.

Next moment, the two infantrymen levered their bayonets into the side panelling of the last door to bar their way. They grunted with the effort. For a moment nothing happened. Then with a sharp crack that made all of them jump, the rusty ancient hinges of the door gave. Swiftly the first of the mouse-holers grabbed the door before it fell inwards. Then, hardly daring to breathe, he and his mate started to edge it open, inch by inch, as if the piece of rotten wood was something infinitely precious. Weak yellow light began to flood into the dark loft.

Mackenzie signalled to the two men to stand a little aside, while he peered into the other room. They did so, happily. Mackenzie pressed his eye to the slit. He caught his gasp of surprise just in time. What he saw was totally, absolutely unexpected. It was something that he could never have imagined taking place at this time and under these circumstances in his wildest of dreams.

A fat naked older woman was propped back in a large

185

chair, her huge breasts thrust forward voluptuously, gasping wildly for breath. Kneeling between her widespread legs, there was another woman, also naked, but much younger, not much more than a child, Mackenzie realized later. And the girl was doing something totally obscene but obviously tremendously exciting to the fat woman. For she was almost out of control. Her breath was now coming in fast shallow gasps, as if she might well be about to die. The sweat was streaming down her gross body and the fat on her thighs trembled in waves. Now her belly was moving in and out in a wild fury as if she had lost control of herself altogether, her teeth bared, as she grated out terrible obscenities. Like dogs on heat, Mackenzie told himself in total disgust, as behind him the Old Sweat, peering through the slit over his shoulder, gasped, 'Well, I'll be buggered . . . it's her!'

'Who?' Mackenzie hissed, still unable to take his gaze off the gross woman, who was now jerking her head back and forth in wild fury, as if she were being choked to death.

'Madame frigging Giselle!'

Four

Fräulein Jacobsohn was tired. She was also feeling vaguely guilty that it was her fault that they had not discovered the identity of the pianist yet. And all the time at the back of her mind there was the nagging thought that her father's life depended upon on the success of their – her – efforts. How, though, the stern-faced Major Dalby was going to save her father, imprisoned far off in an enemy country, was beyond her. But at the moment she dare not ask. First they had to catch the enemy agent.

All the same, she had every confidence in the Englishman. He seemed to know exactly what he was doing. If, however, she had been able to read Dalby's mind, she wouldn't have been so confident. Dalby knew that time was running out for them – *fast*. That afternoon he had heard on the grapevine that if the navy couldn't stop its grave losses in shipping within the next twenty-four hours, Admiral Ramsey wanted to call off Operation Dynamo. He planned to approach the new Prime Minister, Winston Churchill, and point out to him that soon the Royal Navy and the Royal Air Force would be in the front line if – and when – Hitler decided to invade Britain. The beaten army, what was left of it, would be useless then; it had lost its guns, tanks, heavy equipment, most of the soldiers would be armed with hand guns. Thus everything would be dependent on the two other services and they couldn't afford to lose any more ships or planes.

Now since morning, they had been telephoning every

signal Corps operative, keeping the man in question chatting, while she sat listening on the extension, and tried to recognize the voice of the pianist. But all of the signallers they called seemed to possess what she termed 'country accents'. Not one of them seemed remotely like the voice she had heard in the chain locker.

So they took a break now. They sat in Dalby's temporary office in the castle, sipping too strong tea, laced in his case with scotch, while Dalby tried to encourage her with the latest news from Dunkirk. 'Just received a signal from Mackenzie. He's got the woman and some of her fellow . . .' He grunted and instead of 'whores', which he had intended to say, he added, 'ladies of the night.'

All the same, the young Jewish girl shuddered a little at the memory of Madame Giselle that night when the former had approached her, naked, drunk and rapacious, with that horrible rubber thing thrusting out and trembling from within her hairy loins.

'I'm glad,' she responded. 'But I don't know how much she will help us, Major. She will not co-operate easily. And as for me, I am not any great help either.' She shrugged and lapsed into silence.

For a while the two of them sat there without exchanging a word: the veteran, middle-aged soldier and the fragile, hurt, young Jewish girl, both wrapped up in a cocoon of their own brooding thoughts. Outside over the Channel, the Stukas were falling shrieking from the blue sky yet once again. Like evil metal hawks they raced to the water before levelling out at the very last moment, a myriad of evil, black eggs, which were bombs, tumbling out of their pale blue bellies. Below, another civilian craft packed with soldiers who had just escaped the horrors of Dunkirk was now faced with new horrors just when they were in sight of safety here at Dover.

Obviously the sight of the craft being straddled by bombs,

momentarily obscured by huge gouts of whirling white water, lent new impetus to Dalby's thinking. He came out of his reverie abruptly to remark, 'You're right, Fräulein Jacobsohn. We've nothing more to work on than these bloody long-winded phone calls. They take too long, as it is. In essence, with the little time now at our disposal, we've got to force him into the open like you might a fox during a hunt. We've got somehow to scare him into doing a runner.' He paused and his urgent tone vanished mometarily. 'But how? That's the rub.'

She answered the rhetorical question immediately, as if she had been waiting impatiently for it to be asked. 'You know Madame Giselle, whom you are now bringing to Dover?'

'Yes?'

'Well, can't she be the one who makes him get out of that hole of yours, Major?'

'How do you mean?'

'Like this . . .'

'Did you hear, Mick?' Bill said as they sat there, sipping their halves of 'mild and bitter' in the corporals' wet canteen.

'Wish you'd call me by my bloody right name – Tim. But go on with it. Get it off yer chest as the actress said to the bishop.'

Bill looked around, but their fellow men, like themselves, were too busy with their beer to be concerned at what was going on at the other tables in the smoke-filled canteen. Besides, *Garrison Theatre* was on the radio and Enoch's loud north country voice was drowning out most of the other sound.

'Don't be shirty, Paddy,' Bill said with a grin, deliberately needling his fellow NCO. 'Anyhow, it came over the wire this afternoon just after you went off shift. They're bringing some sort of Frog Mata Hari back here to the castle from Dunkirk.'

Kerrigan caught himself just in time, otherwise he might well have cried out loud with shock. There could be only one 'Frog Mata Hari' worthy of sending a patrol across to capture and risk the sinking of whatever craft was bringing her at this moment to Dover – Madame Giselle, or that Flemish mare of a lesbian schoolteacher he had got to know the previous year when he had been in a still neutral Belgium.

'Well, from what I hear, old mucker, this Frog dame has been giving away the details of our shipping to Dover to the Jerries so that they could sink 'em. You can betcha she'll be for the frigging high jump once they've gotten her back and pumped her dry of what info she knows. They'll string her up high, though what I hear there's plenty o' meat on her. Old Pierrepoint, the hangman, will have his work cut out.' He chuckled happily. 'Bit o' waste of all that trained cunt though, don't yer think, Mick?'

From what appeared to be a long way off, he heard himself agreeing with the cruel sentiment.

A few moments later he drained the rest of his half and went. Afterwards he didn't remember what excuse he made to leave so hurriedly, even turning down the offer of 'the other half, on me, mate . . . It's my turn to push the boat out, Mick.' But he went and five minutes later he was in his little room, staring at and talking to himself in the shaving mirror, frantically wondering how he was going to make his escape, for he knew now that the time had come at last for him to run.

He was armed with his little Walther automatic and he had plenty of what he called his 'mad' or 'escape money': nearly two thousand pounds' worth in big crisp white fivers. He knew that kind of money would buy him a lot of favours. But what good would it do him if he went to ground in this damned England? After all, the place *was* an island. Sooner or later the authorities would catch up with him as they had done with the 'boys' after the Easter Rising (as the English swine called it) in Dublin back in 1916.

He saw the sweat standing out like opaque pearls on his forehead in the mirror and his heart was beating furiously like a trip hammer going all out. The stress. He forced himself to be calm. He had to think of a way. Panic would do him no good.

Then he had it. His thinking had been in the wrong direction. He had been pondering going to ground within the damned English island. That was wrong. His friends were only twenty miles away on the other side of the Channel. For all he knew they were massing for their final attack on Dunkirk at this very moment. His work here was, to all intents and purposes, over. What he needed to do to make a successful escape was to head for Dunkirk. In the general confusion of the panic-stricken English, surely it couldn't be too difficult to get on one of the many crafts, most of them manned by civvies, heading for the French port?

Hastily he set about his preparations for his flight, his mind made up in a matter of minutes. Naturally once they had discovered his identity, they'd search his room looking for his *Abwehr* transmitter. He grinned cynically. Well, he'd give them something to surprise the buggers. Swiftly he unfolded the pack of four blankets which regulations prescribed should be made up thus during duty hours. He took the little transmitter from its hiding place and tucked it into the middle of the pack, activating the self-destruct button at the same time. Then he made up the blankets neatly as before, placing his spare pair of boots, instep polished as required, and gleaming mess tins against the pack. For a moment he admired his handiwork. It looked like the effort of a good conscientuous soldier, who didn't mind 'bulling' up his equipment one bit. Then he started working on his

191

battledress blouse, swiftly wielding the needle and thread taken from his 'housewife'*.

It was while he was thus engaged that the tannoy in the corridor outside boomed into metallic life to state, 'All Royal Signals personnel will report immediately to the office of the Chief Signals Officer at once. There will be no exceptions. Out.'

He smirked. They couldn't fool him. He knew exactly what they were about. They were trying to smoke him out. But they had another think coming. He bit through the last of the thread and admired his handiwork once again. The stripes and the flash of the Royal Signals had disappeared. In their place was the red infantry flash of the West Kents, while now the epaulettes bore the three pips of a captain.

He was pleased with his image in the mirror. Who would stop him? Besides, who in his right mind would be wanting to go to Dunkirk now when it was about to fall into German hands at any minute? So he didn't have the right papers. What did it matter? No civvie was going to question him when he boarded the man's craft. He was being rushed to Dunkirk to take over an infantry company on the perimeter which had lost all its officers. Why, wasn't he a brave young officer, doing his duty at this desperate hour, probably on his way to a violent death. His cynical grin broadened even more. He took one last look at the little room. Then he turned out the light and stepped into the corridor. Swinging his officer's swagger stick, that happy Irish smile on his handsome face once more, he was so pleased with himself that he almost forgot to return the salute of a flustered clerk in the Army Pay Corps, who made such a production of it that

---

*Name given to a canvas holder containing the soldier's cleaning and mending tackle. *Transl.*

he might well have been the Commander-in-Chief, Home Forces . . .

Some hundred yards away in another corridor, Dalby turned to the Controller of Signals, a captain, and said, 'I'll leave now. Identify your chaps, please. Check if anyone's missing and get back to me with the name of any missing bloke. Take your time. I think our man will have got the message and done a bunk already.' He responded to the captain's salute and turned back to the girl. 'Excellent idea,' he complimented her. 'Naturally our suspect won't walk into the obvious trap. Now he'll be out there somewhere on the street trying to make his escape.'

She returned his smile a little wanly and asked, 'Where do you think he might go, Major?'

He indicated the hill beyond the castle with a nod of his head. 'London possibly. It's easy to get lost in a big city. Or?'

'To the docks?' she suggested. 'He might well make the attempt to get out of England.'

'You're right,' Dalby said after a few moments. His voice rose. 'I think we'll have to look into that possibility right away, Fräulein Jacobsohn.'

She hesitated and then said, 'But you will do your best to save my father won't you, when all this is over, Major?' She looked up at him, her dark eyes brimming with tears.

Dalby was a completely unemotional man. He had been through too much in his life to allow emotions to pay a role in his thinking now. Hurriedly he pressed her skinny cold hand. 'Of course, I will,' he answered confidently. But even as he said the words, he knew he was lying. The problems of the little people like the Jewish girl didn't matter any longer. Now, the first and only priority was the future of Britain.

Five

They were tired, filthy, yet happy. Their mission was finally over at the cost of one man seriously wounded and two of the West Kents lightly wounded. The eager young subaltern had had a narrow escape when snipers had commenced firing at them as they had made their way down to the waiting naval launch: a bullet had slammed into his helmet and for a moment Mackenzie had thought he was dead, but the young officer had escaped with a nasty headache and a gob of spittle dribbling down his shocked features where Madame Giselle had spat at him as he had grabbed her before she could escape.

The Old Sweat had gone into action immediately as she had followed up with an attempt to kick the officer in the groin, crying over the angry snap-and-crack of the small arms battle. 'Now that's not a nice thing for a lady to do,' he had commented as he had grabbed her and pulled her back, swearing and spitting crazily, and given her breasts an extra hard squeeze by way of punishment – or at least he told himself it was some kind of punishment.

Now they relaxed in the June sun on the deck of the launch, drinking strong Sarnt Major's Tea, well laced with rum, waiting for the trucks and ambulances to transport them up to the castle, while the subaltern, still pale from his ordeal with the woman, played the role of the good officer, passing from man to man, asking after their well-being, even distributing his own cigarettes to those who smoked.

Mackenzie was faintly amused. The boy had hardly begun to shave and his first taste of combat hadn't lasted more than a couple of hours, yet here he was, acting like a battle-hardened 'front-line swine'.

For his part, naturally, the Old Sweat wasn't impressed. 'Get an eyeful of him, sir,' he said hoarsely. 'Ain't long outa short pants and he's—' He stopped abruptly and dug a surprised Mackenzie in the ribs.

The latter gasped. Angrily he burst out with, 'What the hell d'you think you're about, eh? Remember I'm an officer . . .' His words trailed away for he could see that the Old Sweat was not listening. Instead, he followed the direction of the latter's open-mouthed gaze.

The Old Sweat was staring at Madame Giselle, who was under the guard of a naval rating with a fixed bayonet and rifle slung over his shoulder. The brothel-keeper, the old Frog Bag, as he called her, was trying to attract the attention of a young infantry officer who was talking urgently to one of the civilian skippers involved in the great rescue operation. The officer was standing further up the quay talking down to the middle-aged bespectacled skipper who was standing, shielding his eyes against the sun, on the deck of his little boat with its outsized 'red duster' flag hanging limply in the slight breeze.

'What d'yer think the old bag's got do with the officer, sir?' the Old Sweat asked urgently. 'And she's shouting some foreign to him—'

'Not foreign,' Mackenzie cut into his words sharply. 'She's speaking *bloody German!*'

Kerrigan knew he'd been rumbled. The two soldiers on the deck of the naval launch were looking at him hard, obviously puzzled, their minds not yet made up, while the Flemish cow kept on shouting at him in her fractured German. But he knew it wouldn't be long before they made up their minds and came across to investigate. Then he'd be really deep in the shit. There'd be no way he could talk his way out of a situation like this one.

He looked hard at the civilian. He looked a typical weekend sailor in his blazer and white flannels, down to the yachting cap set at a rakish angle. 'You can sail at once, skipper?' he demanded.

'In a way, sir . . . but I haven't got my official orders yet.'

'You don't need 'em,' the pianist lied glibly. 'The word is to get over and bring back as many of our poor chaps that you can carry. I have to do the same but –' he managed a smile, but only just, for time was now running out fast – 'in my case, I don't think I shall be coming back so soon.'

'I say, never say die, old man,' the skipper said. 'But . . .' He hesitated. 'I don't know so much about the navy. You know, Senior Service and all that. Very strict about regs . . . Wouldn't like, I suppose, if I just weighed anchor . . .'

Kerrigan was no longer listening to the civilian's drivel. Madame Giselle, the fat cow, was screaming across at him almost hysterically now, her huge breasts trembling like puddings under her blouse with the effort. The two soldiers had left the launch and were coming up the jetty. They were slow but purposeful. Kerrigan looked around for some way out. To his front a staff car was just pulling up. Another officer got out, followed an instant later by a skinny girl. He gasped with shock. It was the Jewess. Things were closing in on him fast. He felt for his automatic. The newcomers had joined the two soldiers. They stopped and talked for a moment or two.

Desperately he bent down to the civilian skipper once more. 'What about moving out now? I'll vouch for you with the Royal. If anyone has to take the can back, it'll be me.'

'I understand, sir,' the civilian answered. 'But there is still the problem of my fuel ration. I've got to get a navy chitty for it after I've got my orders—'

'Fuck you and your fucking orders!' he burst out in blind frustration. '*Und du, du blöde Kuh,*' he bellowed at the shrieking brothel-keeper, '*halt die verdammte Schnauze!*'

Fräulein Jacobsohn swung round. 'It's him!' she cried. 'The voice I heard in the chain locker.'

'Come on,' Dalby commanded. He started to run, fast for a man of his age. The others broke into a run too.

Kerrigan's nerve broke at last. He pulled out the automatic. 'Stand back,' he threatened.

Without waiting for them to obey, he pressed the trigger. The automatic jerked upwards. Flame shot from its nozzle. The girl yelled. She staggered. She seemed to go on a few more paces. The front of her dress started to flush a bright red. Her knees began to crumple beneath her like those of a newborn foal.

'*Hilfe,*' she gasped weakly.

Dalby grabbed for her. Too late. She eluded his grip. She sank to the floor, fighting to keep her head up like a boxer refusing to go down for the count. To no avail. Her head sank on to her blood-soaked dress. Next moment she collapsed completely.

'You absolute swine!' Mackenzie yelled enraged. He jerked up his own revolver.

'*Stop!*' Dalby commanded. 'Don't shoot him!'

Mackenzie wasn't listening. He fired without appearing to aim. At that range he couldn't miss. The impact of the bullet at that short range spun Kerrigan completely round. His knee shattered. The broken bone gleamed like polished ivory against the bright red gore. His automatic dropped from his suddenly nerveless fingers as he stared down at his knee in absolute disbelief that this was happening to him. Then he started to cry bitterly, his shoulders heaving like those of some heartbroken child.

Not for long. Still carried away by a burning rage at the death of the young Jewish girl, Mackenzie launched himself

197

forward like a rugby player, and with all his strength he slammed into the pianist. The latter went down, gobs of rich red blood splattering the civilian skipper's immaculate white cap. Next instant he had blacked out and all around him the others froze like poor actors at the end of the final act in some cheap theatrical melodrama. It was over . . .

ENVOI

If it be life that awaits, I shall live forever unconquered;
If death, I shall die at last strong in my pride and free.

Scottish National Memorial

It was a cold grey overcast morning. Indeed, the Tower of London was shrouded by a soft mist which was rising from the river. It muted the sound of the sentries on the gravelled paths and the soft commands of the NCOs who seemed awed by their surroundings and what would happen here this day.

Dalby and Mackenzie acknowledged the salutes of the sentries – they were Irish Guards – and the token position of attention of the Beefeaters with their pikes. But this morning no one was standing on military ceremony; the occasion was too grave for that, it appeared.

It had started like that at the secret trial the day before. Kerrigan, supported by wooden crutches, had been described as a traitor, pure and simple. Somehow or other the prosecutor had dug up his birth certificate. It proved he had been born a British subject when the whole of Ireland had been part of the British Isles. That had sealed his fate, more than the fact that he had murdered the Jewish refugee in Dover and killed poor Fräulein Jacobsohn, which his pathetic defending officer, a weak-chinned officer from the Welsh Guards with a bad lisp, had tried to maintain had been an act of self-defence – manslaughter at the worst. He had failed miserably to do so.

By the afternoon, after an hour's break for lunch in the officers' mess, the official trial spectators had grown accustomed to the fact that they were trying a man for his

201

life. In fact, the high drama of the would-be Irish rebel, fighting for a cause which had been lost a quarter of a century before, had become boring. Kerrigan had been reduced to an ordinary mortal. Even the fact that he was obviously in great pain from where Mackenzie had shot him was overlooked and people started to wonder what was for dinner and if the mess might be able to produce a decent claret for the main meat dish and a couple of scotches afterwards.

When Kerrigan, in the final summation, asked the court whether he could address the room – he had something to say about a Free Ireland – the chairman of the board, a crusty brigadier-general who had won the Victoria Cross in the Boer War turned him down with a snorted, 'We want none of that treacherous seditious stuff here in the Tower of all places.'

But the crusty old warrior with a great sweeping white Edwardian moustache did allow the defending officer to relate how the accused had worked for the Intelligence Service as soon as they had patched up his wound, and he was well enough to transmit to the *Abwehr* listening station just outside Hamburg.

Listening to the pathetic Guards officer, recounting his client's 'willing co-operation inspite of being badly wounded', Dalby whispered to Mackenzie, 'He's really making a dog's breakfast of it. He doesn't bloody well know the half of it.'

Mackenzie nodded his agreement. The Welsh Guards officer certainly didn't . . .

The explosion had caught the orderly sergeant, who had been detailed to search Kerrigan's quarters, completely by surprise. He reached under the piled biscuits* with his pacing stick and activated the transmitter's self-destruct

---

*A type of short mattress, coming in threes, used in the wartime British Army. *Transl.*

device. The bed had erupted. The detonation had thrown the unfortunate sergeant backwards through the door, tearing off his clothes and slamming him to the floor of the corridor, where he was found semi-conscious a little later by a red-faced ATS trying to pull what was left of his 'drawers, cellular, short' around his naked and somewhat charred genitals.

It was recorded that despite his pain, Kerrigan, being treated in the MI Room for his wound, managed a smile at the news. But when Dalby went to work on him half an hour later, the pianist soon found out that for the rest of his short – very short – life he wasn't going to have much to smile about.

Dalby commenced his interrogation with a no nonsense, 'I'm not going to waste any time on you, Kerrigan. Besides, it's in your own interest to answer my questions in the shortest possible time. The sooner you do, the quicker you'll get proper treatment for your wound.'

Kerrigan looked up at him, eyes filled with tears of pain. 'Fuck you,' he snarled defiantly.

Dalby's expression didn't change one bit; he simply ignored the comment. Instead he continued as if nothing had happened with, 'I ask only one thing of you, Kerrigan. And it's this. You send a single message to Wohltorf, stating –' Mackenzie noted that Kerrigan's look changed momentarily at the mention of the *Abwehr*'s receiving station. It obviously had shocked him to learn that Dalby knew so much – 'the following.'

He unfolded a piece of paper and read out the message that he and Mackenzie and a chinless but very clever major from War Office Intelligence, named Strong, had spent a lot of the night working on. 'Two new divisions to be sent to France, general area south of the Somme. Talk here is that they and troops of Line of Communications already in place will launch a flank attack on German left wing. More armour is being sent to reinforce English 1st Armoured Division.' He finished and folded the paper once more, commenting, 'That's about the length of one of your usual messages sent at your usual transmission speed, isn't it?' He spoke, as if Kerrigan had already agreed to do the job.

Despite the pain of his wound, Kerrigan looked at him aghast. 'You must be . . . out of your mind, Major,' he stuttered. 'You don't bloody well expect me to send that, do you . . . ? Why –' he looked wildly at Mackenzie as if looking for confimation that Dalby had gone stark raving mad – 'that might convince the German High Command to temporarily stop operations against Dunkirk and let more of you damned English—' His protest ended in a howl of sheer agony, as Dalby, his face expressionless, jabbed the end of his swagger stick into the bloody gore of the yet unbandaged wound.

Mackenzie gasped. He hadn't expected that either. Dalby was definitely going to pull out all the stops in this case. No wonder he had just asked the MO attending to Kerrigan's shattered knee to leave the MI Room. He wanted no witnesses to what was, to all intents and purposes, torture.

'I don't care what you think, Kerrigan,' Dalby continued in the same toneless, unemotional manner as before. 'I don't care either how you hurt. You're a dead man already, remember. But while you're still alive, I'd advise you to do as I say, if you want to die painlessly and at peace.'

'But this is the twentieth century,' Kerrigan protested hotly. 'You don't – can't – torture people like that.'

'Tell that to your people who run the concentration camps,' Dalby answered and laughed cynically.

For a moment Mackenzie thought of the dead girl and her unknown father who indirectly Dalby was sentencing to death once he 'convinced' Kerrigan to send that fake message. A moment later he dismissed the ugly thought; it didn't do to dwell on such things now.

Dalby grew serious again. 'You know what gangrene is, Kerrigan?' he asked.

'Of course.'

Dalby didn't seem to hear. He said, as if talking to himself, 'It comes from the Greek, you know. It means gnawing away of the soft flesh. Medically it is the loss of the soft tissue and flesh due to the lack of oxygen. In the Middle Ages, they used to call it the "mortal death". These days, if they can't stop it with drugs, they keep amputating bit by bit, clearing away the decayed flesh, slice by slice, like cutting a prime joint of beef until they can't cut any longer – then you die. But that must be a relief, I should think, after all the minor ops and all that pain, as your legs disappear bit by bit until you're a legless cripple tormented by excruciating agony . . .'

His voice trailed away to nothing, while Kerrigan looked up at him in horror, before saying, 'But that only happens when the wound is neglected or there is no medical aid available. There are doctors . . .' He stopped suddenly before bursting out with: 'YOU WOULDN'T!'

Mackenzie felt his throat suddenly grow very dry as he waited for Dalby's answer to that impassioned outburst, although at the back of his mind he knew what it would be.

'Of course I would, Kerrigan. I'd do anything to save our army over there. You can rest assured of that.'

With an effort of sheer willpower, Kerrigan pulled himself together, for he knew now that he was dealing with someone just as ruthless as the most fanatical Gestapo man. 'You have no real case against me, you know,' he said quite calmly, voice almost under control once more. 'I shot the girl by accident. As for this Jewish fellow you mention, I know nothing of that . . . I'm just an ordinary Irish patriot who got caught up with something that was bigger than himself.' He flashed a glance at Mackenzie, as if he thought he might

205

have convinced the younger man with his tale. Unknown to him, he had in a way. Mackenzie knew it would take days, perhaps even weeks to set up a convincing, well-evidenced case against the wounded pianist. By then, disaster would have struck what was left of the British Army in France.

But Kerrigan's story cut no ice with a hard-faced Dalby. He clicked his fingers at Mackenzie. 'Bring her in,' he commanded.

Mackenzie opened the door. Madame Giselle burst in, ignoring the loaded revolver that the Old Sweat had pointed at her broad back. Her face was flushed with rage. If she hadn't been handcuffed, Mackenzie could have sworn she would have gone for Kerrigan's face on the spot, ripping and tearing at it with those long sharp whore's nails of hers.

'*Tu sale con!*' she swore violently, spittle flying everywhere. There followed an outburst in Flemish and then in guttural accented German concluding with, '*Ist es alles deine Schuld*' – it's all your fault – '*Du Schweinehund!*'

Dalby shrugged as if her outburst confirmed all he had already said. 'You see, you haven't a chance. She's told us all about your period in Belgium this last winter and the money you got from Admiral Canaris. We know that she and – er – ladies from Dunkirk were supplying you till recently with the details of our ships leaving the port.' He raised and lowered his hands as if there was nothing more to be said. 'On her evidence alone, we could hang you.' He turned to the Old Sweat. 'Wheel her out, please. And watch she doesn't bite you – you might get blood poisoning.'

The Old Sweat grinned and poked his revolver into the irate Belgian woman's back. 'All right, sweetheart, move it.' He looked up at Dalby's slablike face, his own wreathed in smiles. 'Just heard from the adjutant that I'm to be mentioned in dispatches. For bringing them troops back into the perimeter at Dunkirk. Yer know that should be good enough to get me a commission in the old mob. But

I think I'd be better off as an other rank in the Pay Corps, as you promised me, sir.'

Mackenzie grinned and Dalby gave a sigh like a sorely troubled man. 'Don't worry, you little rogue, you'll get your nice cushy posting to the Pay Corps. Now get her out of here before she explodes.'

As the Old Sweat prodded her round with his pistol, she turned and before he could stop her, she had spat viciously right into Kerrigan's deathly pale face; and then she and the Old Sweat had gone.

For a long moment there was silence. Slowly, very slow, Kerrigan wiped the spittle from his face with a hand that trembled badly. Mackenzie could see all the fight had been knocked out of him by the brothel-keeper's unexpected, vitriolic attack. Silently, he handed Kerrigan a towel from the rack to clean his hand. Equally silently, Kerrigan accepted it.

Finally Dalby broke the heavy brooding silence. 'Well,' he said, tonelessly, 'will you do as I say?'

Weakly Kerrigan nodded his head, as if he were too shocked to speak.

Dalby turned to Mackenzie. His face revealed nothing, though there was a sudden gleam – it might have been of triumph – in his eyes. 'Bring in the medics, Mac, please. Tell 'em we want him patched up for zero thirteen hundred hours.'

'Sir.' Mackenzie turned and went out swiftly. Behind him, Dalby took out his flask and poured some scotch into the silver tumbler. Now *his* hand shook as he did so. He didn't offer any to Kerrigan.

Outside Mackenzie leaned against the door for a moment. We've won, a little voice at the back of his brain crowed in triumph. WE'VE BLOODY WELL WON. Then he pulled himself together and hurried off to find the medical officer and his nurse . . .

*   *   *

207

It was only after the war that Major Mackenzie, as he was now, found out that that last transmission of the doomed pianist had affected the course of history. In that far-off summer of victory in 1945, he was attendant to the interrogation of Field Marshal Gerd von Rundstedt, who had been the General-Officer-in-Command of the German Army Group intent on taking Dunkirk in 1940.

By 1945 von Rundstedt, incredibly wrinkled and given to too much cognac, was very feeble and could only walk with the aid of two sticks. But his mind was quick and vital; and when the question of Dunkirk was mentioned, he took up the subject immediately. 'To me,' he quavered angrily in his thin reedy old man's voice, 'it was one of the great turning points of the war. I can tell you, *meine Herren*, that if I had had my way, the English wouldn't have got off so lightly at Dunkirk. But my hands were tied by direct orders from Hitler himself. While the English were clambering into their boats off the beaches, I was kept uselessly outside the port unable to move.' He coughed thickly and Mackenzie could hear the fluid in his old lungs swish back and forth.

Hastily the chief interrogater signalled for the orderly with the cognac bottle and he himself poured a glass and handed it to the Field Marshal personally with: '*Zum Wohle, Herr Generalfeldmarschall.*'

The old soldier accepted it gratefully and in the style of the old German Officer Corps raised the glass to the third button of his tunic, elbow at a right angle and drained it in one gulp. '*Danke*,' he gasped and then continued, 'I naturally recommended to Supreme Command that my five Panzer divisions should drive immediately into Dunkirk and destroy the English totally.

'My wish was not accorded to. The Führer personally directed that under no circumstances was I to attack. Indeed, I was expected to keep my forward elements at least ten kilometres from Dunkirk. Why?' He laughed scornfully. 'I'll tell you. Because of that old fool, Father Christmas.' He threw a glance at the chief interrogator to check whether he understood.

Swiftly the Chief Interrogator said, 'Yes, we know who he was – Admiral Canaris.'

'Well, he had received information, so he told the Führer that you English were about to launch a four or five divisional attack at our left flank. He had the stupid information from his agents in England.'

Major Mackenzie's heart leapt when he heard the information. They – he and the dead Major Dalby – had always guessed their ploy had worked and had saved the BEF in France. Now he knew it had, for sure, from Germany's most senior soldier.

Rundstedt sighed. 'It was an incredible blunder, due to Hitler's reliance on Canaris' so-called secret agents. If the Führer had actually wished to spare Gort's army*, he couldn't have done a better job. The victory over England had been thrown away.' The old field marshal looked around at the circle of Intelligence officers, as if they were his own staff officers whom he was treating to a high-level insight into the conduct of the war. 'Defeat of England at Dunkirk would have meant that America would not have had a base to launch its 1944 attack against Europe which, as you know, ended in defeat for German arms. Victory at Dunkirk for Germany would have seen the war end in 1940.' The field marshal's wrinkled face seemed to crumble even more, as if he had just realized the significance of his words. Suddenly he appeared to be very old indeed and for a fleeting moment Mackenzie felt sorry for Germany's greatest soldier of the twentieth century, now fated, it seemed, to spend the rest of his life in enemy captivity. But only for a fleeting moment as

---

*Lord Gort, commander of the BEF. *Transl.*

he remembered that it was von Rundstedt who represented the state which had sent poor Fräulein Jacobsohn and her father to their deaths.

But on this grey morning in 1940, with the ships' sirens on the fog-bound Thames wailing like the cries of lost children, Mackenzie knew nothing of the full impact of the double-cross action into which the pseudo-Irishman Kerrigan had been forced. For this morning he and his chief, Major Dalby, were going to be part of the official witnesses to the final chapter in the case of the pianist.

Now, as the two of them, dressed in their best uniforms, marched solemnly in step next to the young captain of the Irish Guards who was in charge of the firing squad, they could hear the muted but rich tones of John McCormack singing in that delightful Irish brogue of his, which had made him so popular all over the United Kingdom.

'Danny Boy,' the guards officer confided out of the side of his mouth. 'He requested it to go with his last breakfast earlier on. Hope it doesn't affect the men. Good tough soldiers that they are, my Micks are a sentimental lot.'

'Sentimental rubbish,' Dalby snapped. 'Never be fooled by all that Irish twaddle, Captain.'

The guardsman made no comment. Mackenzie, who was becoming harder and more cynical by the day under Dalby's tutelage, told himself that the old man was being a little hard on a man who was soon about to die. But like the guards officer, he made no comment.

Abruptly McCormack's rendering of *'the pipes . . . the pipes are calling'* was cut off and a harsh, bass voice commanded, 'Prisoner and escort will form up!' There was a sudden stamping of feet and slapping of hard hands against rifle butts. Along the inner wall between the Constable and Martin Towers where the miniature rifle range was situated, a door was opened. A moment later a squad of six guardsmen, wearing the shamrock of the Irish Guards on their peaked caps, marched out. Behind them came a limping Kerrigan, head bowed, a rosary between his clasped hands, supported by a regimental chaplain, reading from his breviary.

Over and over again, Mackenzie could hear the same old ritual: 'In the name of the Father, the Holy Ghost . . .' Still the words and the scene sent a cold shiver down his spine. For a moment, he felt himself tremble. He feared he might fall. For although he knew that Kerrigan deserved what he was soon going to get, he felt overawed by the scene and wished he would not have to view it any longer. That wasn't to be. Gruffly, Major Dalby said, 'Come on, Mac, let's see the end of this business. Then, God willing, we can have a bloody stiff drink, even if it's not yet ten.'

As the chapel clock sounded ten, the young guards captain stood to the side of the firing squad. The prisoner had refused a chair or a blindfold, but they had tied him to the traditional stake, with the bullet deflector shield behind him. Now the priest-chaplain gave the pianist his final blessing and absolution.

'Stand back, Padre!' the officer commanded, his voice harsh and abrasive, as if the strain was too much for him, too.

He looked at the guardsmen.

Mackenzie tensed.

'Squad!' he cried, voice echoing and re-echoing in the long, low-roofed range. 'Take aim.'

He waited an instant, then ordered 'Aim!'

Kerrigan appeared to straighten up, despite the ropes that bound him to the stake. His chin went up proudly, though the tears were pouring down his ashen cheeks.

The officer paused.

Kerrigan burst into speech suddenly. '*Es lebe der Führer,*'

211

he cried fervently in German, in a voice that a shocked Mackenzie hardly recognized.

In the same moment that the officer ordered, 'FIRE', he screamed, 'God bless Ireland!'

Next moment his head slumped down, the blood streaming from the white aiming paper heart that had been placed on his chest. The officer swallowed hard. He said, 'Doctor, please examine the prisoner.'

The doctor who had been standing behind Mackenzie and Dalby hurried forward, his stethoscope already hanging from his neck. With a grunt he knelt below the prisoner who was hanging from the stake, supported by his bonds. He applied the instrument to Kerrigan while the guards captain waited impatiently for his verdict.

It seemed to take a long time, for the guards captain snapped after a moment, 'If he's not dead, Doctor, please stand back so that we can give him another volley.'

The MO took his instrument from one ear and said angrily, 'God, you're damn keen to see the poor chap dead aren't—' He stopped short. Kerrigan had just given a long dire moan. Hurriedly the MO applied his stethoscope once again to Kerrigan's heart. A mere minute. Then he took the instrument from his ears, straightened up, closed the prisoner's eyelids and said quietly, 'There'll be no need for another volley. He's dead now.'

Dalby nudged Mackenzie, 'Come on, our job's finished. Let's have a stiff drink.'

The mess steward, in his immaculate white jacket, beamed at the two officers, although they weren't members of the Brigade of Guards. 'There's an egg apiece this morning, gentlemen,' he announced like a fawning head waiter offering a special treat to honoured guests. 'There's always something like that – on days like this.'

Dalby wasn't impressed. 'Bring us a bottle of scotch,' he ordered, 'and put it on this officer's bill.' He indicated

Mackenzie. 'After all, you haven't treated me to a drink since you've been commissioned.'

The steward hesitated and looked at the wall clock, as if indicating it was a bit early for such strong waters.

Dalby caught the look and snapped, 'Let's move it, sergeant. I want to hear the repeat of Mr Churchill's last night's speech on Forces Radio.

'Yessir,' the steward said, deciding the hard-faced major of Intelligence was not a man to be crossed or kept waiting.

Five minutes later, with Dalby puffing at his old pipe, the two of them were relaxing in the battered leather armchairs of the mess, waiting for the Churchill broadcast to commence. Dalby was saying reflectively between puffs at his smelly old briar, 'You know, Mac, we've seen part of a great British Army run away, with some of it becoming a ruddy undisciplined rabble. In the last show I saw Gough's 5th Army break up, but it was nothing like what happened in France.' He took another puff at his pipe and followed it with a sip at his whisky.

Mackenzie said nothing. He could see just how serious the old man was and just how worn and tired; the last weeks had taken it out of him.

'I hope I never shall see anything like it again as long as I live. At times it almost broke my heart to see a British Army like that.' He cleared his throat. 'We shall do what little we can do – and we'll have to be bloody hard, I can tell you. Fair play and all that so-called English decency will have to go out of the window. I've never had kids, you know, Mac. The missus couldn't have 'em and now it's too late. But you're young and randy enough. You'll have 'em undoubtedly.'

Mackenzie laughed a little uncertainly, but he could see that the old man was not really in a joking mood.

'But I want those kids of the future, Mac, to be proud of

213

what we – all of us – have tried to do this year. That is, if they ever want to know, which I doubt. No matter – *we'll* know. It's going to be hard, Mac, bloody hard, and we've got to be hard, too. There's no room for sentiment as with that pseudo-Irishman they've just shot. Our first concern is England and the English –' he forced a little laugh – 'and perhaps the Jocks and the Taffies as well, I suppose.' His face hardened again. 'But remember this, Mac, even when I've gone. The kid gloves. The Hun fights dirty . . . We've got to fight even dirtier. Is that clear?'

'Yessir,' Mackenzie snapped.

Then the mess steward came in to announce, 'Sir, I'm turning on the Forces Radio . . . The PM's broadcast of last night is about to be repeated.'

'Thank you, Sergeant,' Dalby said and began pouring himself another scotch. 'Wheel on our new leader, please.'

The new prime minister began almost thoughtfully, 'We must be very careful not to assign to this deliverance the attributes of a victory . . . Wars are not won by evacuation.'

Dalby nodded his approval and then sat motionless, as did Mackenzie, both glued to the old man's nineteenth-century, old-fashioned rhetoric. But old-fashioned as Churchill's speech was, it was stirring stuff and for the first time since they had become involved in the Dunkirk business, Mackenzie began to feel a sense of hope. Inside his head a cynical little voice sneered, It's the whisky, old man. He ignored the voice and continued to listen, while opposite him, sunk in thought, Dalby smoked and drank.

Outside, the clanging bell of the ambulance indicated it had arrived to take away the body of the dead Kerrigan. It'd take the body away to be buried in an unmarked grave at the East London Cemetery at Plaistow. At this perilous juncture in the war, no one should know that there were traitors in their midst here in the heart of the British Empire.

'. . . we shall not flag or fail,' Churchill was declaring, his voice firm, full and determined. 'We shall go on to the end . . . We shall fight on the seas and the oceans . . . we shall fight on the beaches, we shall fight on the landing grounds, we shall fight in the fields and in the streets, we shall fight in the hills; we shall never surrender . . .'

The poignancy of Churchill's words was almost unbearable. In the pause which the PM now made to catch his breath, Mackenzie threw a quick glance at Dalby. His chief was smiling, yet two large tears were, at the same time, coursing down his worn pale face. Mackenzie could understand why. In years to come whenever he thought of his long dead old chief he'd always remember him at this moment, his patriotic soul laid bare at the memory of Britain's recent earth-shaking defeat, but with new hope suddenly animating his tired body.

Suddenly Churchill trumpeted out his last sentence. It hit Mackenzie like a blow from a clenched fist. It was: 'WE SHALL NEVER SURRENDER!' In that glorious, electrifying moment, Mackenzie knew they never would . . .